NOVEMBER RAIN

BY SUN STARS

"And when your fears subside
And shadows still remain, oh yeah
I know that you can love me when there's no one left to blame
So never mind the darkness, we still can find a way
'Cause nothin' lasts forever, even cold November rain."

~Guns N' Roses

Sun Stars

November Rain

Self-published through NiteSun Publishing

(thesunstars@live.com)

PREFACE

Trey and Andrew: The loves of my existence
Momma: The strongest woman I ever knew
Amanda: My soul sister, my best friend, the one who knows me better than anyone
Glenda: My sister, my ride or die, the sister I laugh with, enjoy life with.
Casper: For the late night cuddles, the kisses and for all the times you've made me laugh.
Tracy: For being my friend through it all.
Michelle: For never thinking I was the weird girl at the WalMart
Char: For always reminding me how important it is to keep writing.
Shauna: For never letting me forget how important it is to make the reader feel something.
Laurie: Forever my friend!

~Author's Note:

This book means so much to me. My mother passed away from AML and I was a young cancer patient many years ago. Nights in the hospital turn into weeks which turn into months. Loneliness sets in and you start to lose yourself after a while. Writing this book brought up a lot of memories, some good, some bad, all needed.

Dedicated to all the kids (and adults) fighting cancer, especially the ones who feel alone and lost. Keep Fighting.

I was four the first time I experienced death. Not my own, but someone close to me, and it scared me but I was intrigued at the same time. I wanted to know what happens to us when we die. Do we just stop existing? Or do we wind up in Heaven like my mom told me my grandpa was? And how did she know that was where he went? Was it a guarantee that he went to Heaven because my mom said so?

I had so many questions and I wasn't quite sure how to ask them. The only thing I really knew and understood about death at that time was that it made my mom cry and I didn't like when she cried.

I'm seventeen years old now and I'm even more curious about what happens to us after death.

Not because I'm some freak or goth, though I guess you could say I'm both and neither, but because death is stalking me. At least that's how I like to phrase it anyway.

Maybe I should start with why I'm so fascinated with where we end up.

Hi, I'm November and I have cancer. I guess you could say that I'm somewhere between life and death right now because to be honest, I don't know if I'll live through the day much less wake up tomorrow, but that part doesn't scare me. I'm terrified of the unknown. Where will I be? Will I still be able to feel the love I have for people? Or does it all just fade away like some distant memory that is lingering on the edges of my brain and I just can't recall it?

Having cancer isn't a death sentence these days. I know that's what most of you are thinking. But when you've been fighting it since you were eleven, you start to wonder if maybe it is the way you're going to die.

I was diagnosed with AML, or acute myeloid leukemia when I was eleven years old. I'd been sick for a few weeks and my mom was getting tired of me not wanting to get up for school and when I came home every day and took a nap, she finally decided to take me to a doctor. I was given iron pills and told I was anemic and sent home.

Three days later, I walked in the front door after school to find my mom sitting at the kitchen table crying. I had no idea what was happening but I knew that I didn't like seeing my mom cry so I hugged her and she cried harder.

It wasn't until after dinner that I found out what was really going on. She called me into the den and her and my dad broke the news to me.

"You start chemo tomorrow."

Those words didn't mean anything to me then. I was just a kid. I didn't really know what chemo was. I knew that kids my age were supposed to go to school, do homework, maybe play a sport or two and otherwise behave but this chemo thing was all brand new to me.

Flash forward six years and I'm an old pro at chemo now. I know that it destroys the cancer cells but kills all the good cells too along the way. It makes me lose my hair and feel like I'm dying but I'm not, thanks to the chemo. At least that's what the nurses keep trying to tell me.

This is my fifth round here with relapse. This time is different. This time, I really may die and I'm not so sure I'm ready just yet.

The last few rounds with this dreaded disease were okay. Or as okay as having cancer can be. I went into remission each time and those remissions lasted six months to a year each.

This last round, I never went into remission. This cancer has grown more aggressive and we are running out of options. I'm worn down physically and mentally and I'm tired. Tired of cancer. Tired of living. Tired of dying. I'm just.........tired.

My mom tries to put on a brave front. She's always smiling and laughing with the nurses when she's here.

And she's always here. She quit her job after my first relapse and never left my side for the entire month I was in this hospital. I don't know how or why she did that but I was so grateful to have her by my side. I was scared and I just wanted my mom. And she didn't let me down.

Now.....well now is a completely different story. She comes and goes but she's here more than she isn't. To be honest with you, I'd rather she not be here at all. I can't stand listening to her little speeches about how strong I am or how brave I'm being. I'm her hero. Some hero, right? I can't even kick cancer's ass.

Today I start another round of poison. It will slowly drip and flow through my veins as my blood carries it to whatever battlefield it needs to be at now. The cancer will fight back.

And it's winning.

This is my third cycle of chemo this round. I get daily blood transfusions now and platelets at least once a week just so I have the strength to keep fighting when in reality I don't want to fight anymore.

I want to close my eyes, go to sleep and just die. It has to be better than this life I have now. No life is better than a life lived inside these yellow walls of this hospital room.

I'm a senior in high school but I haven't actually seen the inside of my school since I was a freshman. I've spent all of my time on homebound, taking classes in the hospital or at home with a special teacher who helps me try to remember the details of stupid crap like the French and Indian War or some made up nonsense about dinosaurs. What good is that doing me? It's not like I'm going to live long enough to actually go discover if dinosaurs were even real.

The only war I care about is the War of Cancer and November. And while I'm complaining, what the hell was my mother thinking naming me November Rain Collins? Dad says it's because she had a big old crush on Axl Rose when she was younger. Mom always huffs at him and they both laugh when he says it. I think I'll miss them the most when I'm gone.

I know that most kids my age aren't close with their parents, at least not the way that I am with mine. Most kids my age haven't spent months on end with just their parents for company either like I have. I always feel bad for them because they only have me and my sister and what happens if I die? Do they just stop being a mom and dad? Or do they keep going but tell everyone that their kid is dead now?

It's a lot to think about and to be completely frank with you, I'd rather be thinking about what college I'm trying to get into or who I'm gonna screw this weekend.

But that's not what the Universe had in store for me, so here I am, lying in this hospital room, staring at the garish yellow walls of room 301 for the nine thousandth day in a row. I'm used to the smells here now. Like how the hallways smell of disinfectant and room 342 always smells like old people because that's where they put the terminally old when they come in for a stay.

The nurses always play rock paper scissors for who has to deal with room 342. I wonder if they do that when they know I'm coming back? I can be a pain in the ass I'm sure. I'm demanding and I get angry a lot. I have a lot to be angry about.

Personally, I think room 342 is haunted and that's why no one ever survives their stay in it. Someday, I'm going to be in room 342.

And I won't leave it alive.

Chapter 2

It's Friday, and that means that Dad will be staying the weekend here with me. Funny how you get to know the routine so quickly when you're stuck in a bed in a hospital. Dad staying means that the nurses will come by more often because my dad is kinda hot. We'll walk the halls more because I can't say no to my dad. Not since I found him crying one night when he thought I was sleeping. He wasn't just crying though, he was praying. He asked God to let him take the cancer that was killing me so that I would have a chance to experience life outside of the hospital. He sounded scared and alone and I pretended to still be asleep so he wouldn't feel bad about crying.

My dad crying nearly killed me. Not in a literal sense because only cancer was doing that but in an emotionally bankrupt kind of way. My heart hurt knowing that someday, I would leave him behind and he'd blame himself.

I was still thinking about this when he breezed into the room with a big smile and an even bigger bag of food.

"Hey, kiddo, got your favorite," he said, dropping the McDonald's bag on my tray table. He was already pulling nuggets and fries out before I could laugh.

"What the heck, Dad? Did you think that we'd starve?" I playfully rolled my eyes at him and he laughed, still pulling food out of the bag. "And tonight is the good hospital food. Thanks to you I'm gonna miss the fish."

We both laughed so loudly at that that my nurse stuck her head in the room to find out what the joke was. Dad offered her a double cheeseburger before she hurried off to check on her other patients.

"So, November, what game did you pick out for tonight?"

Fridays were game night for Dad and I and he never skipped game night. Even when I begged to just watch tv. He always said "November, one day you're going to miss playing these games with your old dad" and so we played some random game he'd purchased when I first started staying weeks in the hospital.

"How about Monopoly?" It was his favorite and tonight I just wanted to make Dad happy.

"Oh, my fave." He took a big bite of his Big Mac and grinned at me.

I popped a mcnugget in my mouth and nodded.

Two hours later we were in the midst of a very intense game of real estate when the IV therapist came in to draw some blood.

"Look, kiddo, it's the vampires here to take your blood again."

I rolled my eyes at my father and shook my head. He'd been calling them vampires since I was eleven and first got sick. I was scared of them so much that he'd had to make it a game for me and my dad has such a good heart that he'd continued trying to make me less scared all these years later.

The IV therapist laughed and made fangs with her fingers before getting down to business. Dad was rolling the dice, and moving his little shoe around the board and I glared at him.

"Hey, no cheating. You landed on St. James and you owe me rent."

He huffed and puffed but handed over the fake bills and I tucked them in my PJ pocket. I was losing and we both knew it but my dad would never allow me to feel bad about this stupid game.

"Monopoly can go for days," he said an hour later. "Wanna pick this back up tomorrow night?"

I tried to hide a yawn, and nodded. "Can we watch a movie? Something funny?"

"Sure thing," he said, already getting up and plugging in my laptop so we could find something to watch on HBO Max. We ended up choosing to watch Back To The Future and my dad's laughter filled the room making me smile. I fell asleep a few times but he never said a word. He let me sleep, because I needed it and because while I slept it meant that he didn't have to put on that brave face that said I was going to be okay and survive this.

We watched until late in the night, laughing and dozing off from time to time. I worried about my dad. In the last month, the wrinkles around his eyes had grown deeper and the sadness lingered a little longer each time he caught me staring at him. He knew something that I didn't and I wasn't surprised that my folks would keep things from me.

Around 3a.m., my nurse, Cynthia poked her head in to check on us and tossed a bag of chips my way. My dad accepted her offer of a bottle of water and when she returned, Cynthia took my vitals, smiling when they were normal.

I liked Cynthia. She was kind and quiet but always willing to help me out when I needed it. She would wash my hair and help me bathe when I asked. I was lucky to have her and I told her so often.

Morning came early and my mom and little sister, Tracy, arrived with more games and some magazines to help me pass the time. My mom still thought that magazines were the answer to boredom and Tracy and I shared a quick glance of annoyance before she handed me my iPad.

"Thanks, Trace." She was only two years younger than me but she seemed so much wiser than her years. I guess having a sister who was dying would do that to a kid. There was so much I wanted to share with her, to tell her about life and death.

"You're welcome, November."

A part of me hated her because she had a normal name, even if my mom swore she named her after Tracy Morgan. He was a country singer that she loved but I think she just liked the name and didn't want to saddle another daughter with an unusual moniker.

Tracy sat down in one of the chairs in the room and looked bored. I was sure she would have rather have been anywhere else but here and I didn't blame her one bit. I didn't want to be here either but at least I wasn't forced to be when I could have been at home still sleeping or out with my boyfriend.

Not that I had a boyfriend but Tracy did and I was jealous of that. Someone loved my sister that didn't have to and she deserved it but it was something I would most likely never experience.

My mom was still talking to my dad about the washer not working and I could hear the stress in her voice because they didn't have the money to pay for a new one thanks to my medical bills. We weren't poor by any means but weeks on end in the hospital added up quickly and insurance would only pay so much.

I tuned out again and focused on the news program on the tv mounted on the wall. War in the Ukraine had to be better than living in this hospital while my parents talked about how my disease was draining them financially

They were still discussing it when lunch arrived along with my weekend day shift nurse Pam. She was one of the best but only here every other weekend. I was fairly certain that she sensed my annoyance because she suggested that my family take a break and go out for some lunch while I was set up for next week's round of chemo.

Mom argued for a few minutes before Dad saw my face and pulled her out of the room. Tracy waved bye as she followed behind and I shot Pam a grateful smile.

"Family troubles, love?"

I shrugged. "They mean well."

"Most people do." She nodded at me and set about flushing my IV port. "It's just as hard on them." She rolled her eyes then winked at me. "I call bullshit. You're the one living through these treatments. Yeah, it's hard on them but they can walk away from it all and be normal for the rest of the day."

"Lucky." It was all I could manage and held back tears. Pam was right. I couldn't walk away from cancer and be normal. I would forever be the girl who had cancer and that wasn't who I wanted to be. Not that I knew who or what I wanted to bo. When I was four I wanted to be a princess and a mermaid. Thanks, Disney.

Now, I guess I just wanted to be alive in a year. I hadn't thought about a career since I was fourteen and no one had asked me about one since before then.

I was still thinking about that when the chaos started in the hallway near the nurses desk. It was so loud that both Pam and I turned to see what was happening. She hurried from the room, slamming my door shut behind her and I was annoyed that I had no clue what was causing all of the nurses to be in such an uproar.

Alone in my room, I lay back and scrolled through facebook on my iPad for a bit before I got bored. I swung my legs from the bed and slipped my feet into the slides by my bed. Grabbing the IV pole I drug it along beside me and made my way to the door. I opened it slowly, listening for Pam or some other nurse to yell at me to get back into bed. When that didn't come, I slipped out of the room and hurried down the hall towards the nurses station.

I'd just turned the corner when our eyes met, his blue and angry, mine green and curious. This tall, thin guy was what all the fuss was about and I was desperately curious about him. He just stood there, still yelling, but his gaze fixated on me. I absently smoothed my hair and smiled shyly.

He was beyond cute and my heart was racing but there was no way in Hell I was going to let him know that. I rolled my eyes at his yelling and turned back toward my room. I took my time down the hall, still listening to his demands. Someone should probably tell him this was a hospital and not some hotel that catered to our every whim. Maybe then he would settle down and get better so he could get out of here and things could go back to normal.

I made it back to my room and climbed back into bed just as Pam appeared.

"Where you going, love?"

"Nowhere, I just got back."

"Ah, wanted to see who was making all that noise, did ya? His name is Wyatt and he's new."

"What's he in for?" I was way too curious for my own liking but I needed to know.

"Can't tell ya that, love. But....he's close to your age and he's gonna be needin' a friend. Maybe you could show him the ropes and help him settle down."

"I doubt he wants me to be popping up at his door and telling him the law of the land at Oak Meade Memorial Hospital."

Pam shrugged and jotted a few notes on a piece of paper and waved on her way out. She was right though, he was going to need a friend if he was going to be here for any amount of time.

"Wyatt," I said out loud. It felt odd on my lips but I said it again just to hear it. I really wondered why Wyatt was here. Was he sick sick or just here for a surgery or some illness that would run its course in a few days? Would he understand how life and death played out here at OMMH? Maybe I would stop in and say 'Hi' tomorrow when my dad left for the morning. Sundays were the only days I actually had to myself thanks to my parents going to church. They were pretty fanatical about it to be honest.

I didn't really understand it, but if it helped them to believe that my soul would go to Heaven when I die, then I'm glad they had whatever being they believed in. Personally, I didn't believe. It wasn't that I thought I didn't have a soul. It was that I didn't think it went anywhere when we die.

I used to pray when I first got sick but then I kept getting sick so I started to wonder what the use of prayer really was. To be honest with you, I think prayer is just to make the person praying feel like maybe they have some hope.

I didn't really have a lot of hope lately. I had a lot of questions and a lot of anger and every so often I had a lot of tears but hope wasn't something that was there now.

After Dad returned for the day, we watched a movie and had dinner. Sunday's he ordered pizza in for us and I did my best to eat a full slice of the veggie one he'd ordered. The rest of the evening was spent with Dad reading to me or us talking about school and how I needed to be ready for midterm exams in just a few weeks.

My homeschool teacher didn't come next week due to the chemo schedule but she'd be here the following week and we'd have to focus all of my energy on being ready for those exams if I wanted to do well.

I was determined to graduate on time with the class I'd started with but cancer was always getting in the way. No one would have blamed me if I'd just quit school but I couldn't. It was the one goal that kept me going right now and I was going to graduate even if it killed me in the process.

But first, I had to get through chemo week. I pushed the thoughts away and smiled sleepily up at my father. He leaned in and kissed my forehead and I closed my eyes to sleep.

Chapter Three

A few days had passed since Wyatt was admitted to the hospital and I had talked myself out of going to visit him about a hundred times since. My Dad had left on Monday morning and my mom had been with me all day every day since. I was alone at night this week because Dad was out of town for work and Mom didn't want to leave Tracy home alone. My cousin Tricia had spent the night once but all she did was talk on the phone to her boyfriend so it was like being alone but annoyed by some lame tv show.

Susan, Tricia's mother had stopped by to check on us and they did nothing but fight about how she'd left her dishes in the sink and her room was a disaster. I would have given my left leg for them both to just leave but I had to be nice because my mother would never forgive me if I didn't.

Tonight, Becca was supposed to spend the night but around 6:00 she texted to say she couldn't make it and I breathed a sigh of relief. I was finally getting some time to myself and I was happy about it.

My dinner tray had just been picked up when Wyatt filled my doorway.

"Hey," he breathed and leaned against the doorframe. His smile was awkward and nearly did me in.

"Hey," I tried my best to be cool. I wasn't cool. That was quite evident by the high pitched squeak that they sounded like.

"Wyatt," he said.

"November."

"What the hell kinda name is November?"

I shot him a questioning look and rolled my eyes. "Ask my mom."

"I'm guessing she's a fan of Fall?"

"Nope." I really didn't want to say the next part but I just said it. "Guns N Roses."

"Don't tell me she named you November Rain. I swear I'll ask you to marry me right now."

"Then I guess we're getting hitched."

We both laughed and he finally entered the room and moved the chair closer to my bed. We sat in awkward silence for a bit and then fell into a fight of laughter.

"Welcome to the neighborhood," I said between laughs.

"Thanks, the neighborhood sucks."

"Could be worse. We could be dead."

"Ah Death, the old bastard. He's always creeping around these hallways and peeking in on me in the middle of the night."

He tried to sound unfazed but I heard the fear that hid beneath the words because I felt them too.

"Yeah, he's a pain in the ass."

Wyatt smiled at me and glanced back at the door. I knew he was looking to make sure the nurses weren't about to kick him out. We really weren't supposed to visit one another but it was nice to have him in here.

"Can I ask you a personal question, November?"

"Sure, why not." I didn't really think about it before I answered.

"Are you dying?" He was very serious all of a sudden and so was I.

"Yes."

The silence hung in the air between us like death itself. It was the first time I'd actually admitted it to someone other than myself. I was glad it was Wyatt that asked. Anyone else would have apologized and maybe even cried.

Not Wyatt.

He just sat there with me for a few minutes before he spoke again.

"Guess we got something in common then."

"I have leukemia," I explained. Not that he'd asked, but I felt like I needed to tell him so that he'd understand why I was dying.

"Brain tumor. It's growing pretty fast and it's wound its way through my brain so that removing it is nearly impossible without killing me. So, I'm going to die if they remove it and if they don't."

"How long?" I needed to know.

"A year at most." He shrugged like he didn't care. His eyes told me a different story.

"This is my fifth relapse. No one knows how long I have." I felt the need to let him know that I understood his silent fears. We were alike in that.

"Maybe that's better. Knowing that you're going to die in a year isn't that much fun."

"Knowing you're going to die but not knowing when sucks even more."

"Nah, that's just called life. We are all born dying, November. It's just a matter of when. Not knowing is a part of it."

"I think I'd rather know. This.....lingering isn't fun for anyone." I looked away from him then to hide the tears that threatened to fall.

"It's okay to cry if you need to."

He reached out and took my hand, holding it gently and I let him. He was still holding it five minutes later when Angela, my nurse, came bustling into the room and stopped dead in her tracks.

"Wyatt, what are you doing in here?" She sounded flustered.

"I invited him," I said quickly. "He's new and I figured I'd let him know how things work here."

She sighed heavily and shook her head. "It's not technically against the rules, November, but, we'd prefer that you get permission first. Your blood counts are down and that means you could get sick. We don't need that while you're taking chemo."

"I'm already sick, Angela. Did you forget?"

"Me too," Wyatt chirped in and I shot him a glance that said to shut up and he stuck his tongue out at me causing me to giggle.

"Okay, you two, I'm not going to forbid the visits, but if either of you so much as sniffles, it's over, understood?"

We both nodded and smiled at one another.

"Now, Wyatt," she continued, "it's time for you to go back to your room. I have to get November ready for her next bag and take her vitals. You can come back tomorrow."

"See ya later," he waved on his way out the door.

Angela turned to me after closing the door and curtain and sat on the edge of my bed.

"He's cute, right?"

I shrugged. "I guess."

"Hey, I'm old, not blind. It is okay to like him and it's okay to be friends. Just be careful."

"We're just friends and we're both cancer patients in a hospital. How much more careful can we be?"

She smiled a little sadly and hooked up my IVs before leaving me alone for the night. I spent the remainder of the evening watching The Big Bang Theory reruns and napping. Chemo week always left me exhausted and sick so sleep was exactly what I needed. I woke often but finally turned the lights out around midnight and curled up in my bed and cried for the first time in a long time.

I full on cried for myself being sick and for knowing that I was going to die sooner rather than later. I cried for Wyatt and for my parents. I cried for Tracy and all she would have to deal with when it happened.

I fell asleep with tears still wet on my face but I slept soundly for the first time in weeks. I woke the next morning to find my mother sitting in her chair by the window, working on her crossword puzzles. She smiled and put the puzzle down when she saw I was awake.

"Morning," she said, kissing my forehead. "Breakfast just got here and it looks good today. Let's get you up so you can eat."

"Thanks, Mom."

She helped me sit up in bed and pulled the tray closer so I could nibble at my breakfast. I wasn't feeling well but that was normal when they were pumping poison into my body. I pushed the tray away weakly and Mom frowned.

I knew that the dark circles under my eyes told her all that she needed to know. She helped me brush my teeth in bed and called for a nurse to help her change my clothes. I simply nodded when she chose some different pajamas for me and helped as much as I could. By the time we were done, I was exhausted and fell back to sleep while Mom sat holding my hand.

I slept for hours, through the changing of my chemo IVs, lunch and my aunt calling to see how I was doing. It was starting to get dark when I woke up. Dad was sitting in the chair mom had been in when I fell asleep. I frowned.

"What are you doing here?" I asked weakly.

"Mom said you weren't feeling well, so I cut my trip short."

"Dad," I started and he interrupted me.

"I was happy to get out of there. That conference was boring and the food at the hotel was awful."

"Like hospital food is better?"

"Everything's better when I'm with you, kiddo."

"Thanks, Dad." I smiled up at him and he leaned over to hug me.

"Let's try to get some food in you. I ordered some soup, it should be here any second. Wanna sit up?"

I nodded and pushed the button to move the bed to a seated position while Dad adjusted my pillows. We both expected the knock at the door to be food service but my smile grew wide when it was Wyatt.

"Hey," he said. "I heard you weren't feeling so hot today."

"She's a bit tired," Dad said, throwing a questioning glance my way. "I'm Jim, November's father."

"Wyatt, I'm an inmate here."

Dad laughed and sat back down. "Have a seat, Wyatt. I'm sure November would rather talk to you than me."

"Dad!" I exclaimed in protest.

"It's okay, kiddo. I was young once too. Enjoy some time with your friend."

Wyatt sat in the only other chair in the room and took a deep breath before he spoke again.

"Chemo?"

"Yeah," I said, looking up at the bags on the IV pole. "I hate Chemo week."

"Me too. I start tomorrow so I figured I'd better come see you tonight before I'm comatose too."

"Are your parents coming to stay with you?"

He shook his head. "Nope. They are in Europe, I think. They don't like coming to the hospital when I'm here."

"Oh, I'm sorry." I glanced at my Dad, realizing how lucky I was to have him and my mother be here for all of this. "You can borrow mine if you need to."

Dad just nodded and smiled at us.

"Thanks," Wyatt said. "I might take you up on that."

We sat in the quiet for a bit and I wondered how it felt to know that your family wasn't coming to visit you while you were in the hospital. As many times as I'd wished mine would just go home and leave me alone, I was thankful that they stayed. I wouldn't have survived this long without them by my side every day and night. They were my strength when I had none and they kept me from losing my mind in this place. I worried that Wyatt had no one.

"Do your friends visit you?"

Wyatt seemed startled at the question and took a long time to answer. "Nah, not really. I've been doing this on my own for a while now. My friends are self-absorbed and not good friends to be fair."

"At least you have some. I haven't seen anyone from school since I got sick."

"That's better than friends who don't get that you're sick. They expect me to be able to go out and party. Partying isn't something that matters all that much to me anymore."

I studied his face, and understood the pain I saw reflected there. Being a sick kid meant you didn't get a normal childhood or normal friends who cared to be there when you needed them.

I let the silence engulf us again, unsure of what I should say to make him feel better.

"You find out who your true friends are when you go through things like this, Wyatt." My dad sounded so sure of himself as she spoke. "Kids don't understand when someone their age is facing a life or death crisis. It's hard enough for adults to figure out so I'm sure that your friends don't mean to be insensitive."

"Trust me, Mr. Collins, they do. They weren't good friends before I got cancer. I never expected them to be better human beings when I was diagnosed."

"I'm sorry," I said.

"Don't be sorry, November. I always knew who they were."

I reached out and took his hand in mine. He held mine tightly and we sat quietly again. Dad watched us closely but said nothing. I was grateful for him more than ever that night.

Wyatt stayed another hour or so before my dad suggested it was time for bed for all of us. I wasn't ready to let Wyatt go but I had no choice. He waved once more before he closed the door and I was left with an empty feeling.

I didn't sleep well that evening. I was worried that Wyatt was going to be all alone while he went through treatment. Chemo was hard enough with a support system. It had to be Hell to face it alone.

I couldn't live with the notion that he'd be alone and so I spent the night planning how to be there for him.

The next morning, Angela helped me set up a facetime call with Wyatt just before he started his treatment. He answered with a smile and it made my heart happy to see him.
"Hey, November," he beamed.

He looked like he was ready for battle all propped up on his pillows. I couldn't help but smile as Angela started my own IVs.

"Hey, how are you feeling about today?"

"I'm not sure. I'm not ready for the puking but other than that I guess I'm as ready as anyone can be. How about you?"

"I'm on day four, puking is a given. Try flat Coke, it helps me every time."

"Good tip," he said, turning to look at Toni, his nurse. "Can you bring me some?"

I heard her tell him that she'd make sure he had plenty on hand and I spoke a loud thank you to her over the ipad.

We stayed on Facetime until we both fell asleep. Mom moved the tray table but didn't disconnect the video feed. She deserved a big hug for that and I'd make sure I gave it to her later.

We both woke throughout the day and checked to see how the other was feeling. Wyatt was still feeling okay but day one usually wasn't that bad. Day four on the other hand had him listening to me throw up more than a few times. He handled it well but I could tell he was getting scared for what he was in for.

"Chemo affects us all differently. You may not even get sick."

"Am I gonna lose my hair?"

I ran a hand through my very short brown hair and sighed. "Depends on what chemo you're taking. I'll lose mine soon I'm sure."

"I bet you look hot bald."

I laughed and my mother joined in. She smiled over at me and I knew she was thinking that it was nice that I'd made a friend to help me through all of this even if he was just another cancer kid.

"What can I say," I answered. "I'm hot with or without hair."

Wyatt's laughter filled the air around me and soothed my soul. He was quickly becoming someone I cared about and that scared the crap out of me. I prayed he couldn't see that fear on my face.

We ate lunch together, grilled chicken salad sandwiches and vegetable soup. Neither of us touched our broccoli and my mother protested. She reminded us that we need the extra vitamins while we were taking treatments but we both made yucky faces and shook our heads no.

Wyatt suggested we watch The Kelly Clarkson talk show after lunch and I fell asleep during her interview with Machine Gun Kelly. I would soon learn that Wyatt was a huge fan of MGK and I'd spend far too many hours learning about his music and life.

When I woke up, Wyatt was sleeping and my mother was napping as well. It was late afternoon and Mom would be leaving soon and then it would be just Wyatt and I. For some reason I was nervous. We'd spent every hour talking today but there was something about him that made me feel safe and terrified at the same time.

I knew it was stupid to fall for him and that he most likely didn't feel the same way but falling for Wyatt was inevitable.

Chapter Four

Wyatt and I spent every day on Facetime after that first day. I helplessly watched as he succumbed to the vomiting that came with chemotherapy. I sat quietly while his doctor explained to him how the chemo would help kill the cancer cells but that radiation would be needed to help shrink the tumor itself. I had never needed radiation so I didn't know the side effects. I listened intently when his doctor told him that he'd be more tired than normal, and he'd notice some changes in his skin on his scalp. The doctor explained that he would most likely lose his hair and get sores in his mouth or around it. He warned Wyatt that he would get headaches and should tell the nurses so they could give him something for them. The nausea and vomiting would continue and there was a possibility of seizures with radiation as well.

I was scared for Wyatt but I forced myself to stay strong so that I could help my friend through this. Once Wyatt had fallen asleep again, I asked my mom to help me google all of the possible side effects so I would be prepared for what was to come.

The list was endless it seemed but I needed to be ready so I could help him through this. I refused to be like his other friends. I would be there for him no matter what.

"Honey," my mom cautioned, "don't expect too much. He's sick."

"So am I, Mom. I know what I'm getting into."

"I just don't want to see you get hurt if something happens to him."

I saw the sadness in her eyes and knew that she meant if he died. I hated her for even thinking it but the logical part of me understood that she was right.

"Can you just help me with the American Cancer Society site, so I can help him, please?"

My mother was an angel and did as I asked even though she knew that in the end one or both of us would die and leave the other broken. I knew that she was praying I was the one left broken because it meant that I was alive. It was awful to think that if it came down to me or Wyatt, she'd choose him to die.

I understood it but it broke my heart knowing she'd let him die to save my life. He'd only been in my life a short time but he had started to mean the world to me. Wyatt was my best friend and I didn't even know it then.

I was asleep when Wyatt woke up but his voice brought me awake quickly. My mother was talking to him about how he was feeling and I don't know what he said to her but I became fully awake when she said she'd be right there.

I watched in concern as my mother and two nurses rushed into Wyatt's room. Someone turned the iPad around so I couldn't see anything but I heard him throwing up and dry heaving.

I felt so bad for him but I knew that he just had to deal with it until the medicine kicked in to help him control it. It was miserable but it was what a majority of us had to deal with to kill the cancer that was fighting a war inside of us.

The world wasn't fair and we were on the losing end of it for sure but we also appreciated life so much more. Or I hoped that we did anyway. There were days that I forgot about that appreciation.

My mom walked back into my room like nothing out of the ordinary had happened and said that Wyatt was resting quietly now. The nurse turned the iPad back to face him and I breathed a sigh of relief to see for myself that he was okay.

My last day of chemo was the next day and I was looking forward to that more than almost anything. The following week would be worse than the treatment week but then I'd start to feel better. If my counts went up I may even get to go home and sleep in my own bed again. I wasn't counting on it because every time I did I was disappointed but I still held onto the tiniest shred of hope.

Part of me didn't want to feel better so I could stay here with Wyatt but I knew that wasn't the best thing for either of us. I couldn't count on him being here every time I was sick and he shouldn't count on me either. It was nice to think that we'd stay in touch after this but the reality was that we'd never cross paths again.

I'd made many hospital friends over the years and many of them weren't alive any longer. Some of them got better and moved on with their lives. And then there was me, November, the one who just kept getting sick but wouldn't die.I just sorta lingered. Not well, not dying. I was nothing.

Just sick.

I closed my eyes to avoid my mom and pretended to be asleep. She kissed my cheek softly before she left for the day and I waited a few breaths before I opened my eyes. I was alone again with my thoughts. Dad had gone back to the conference now that he knew it was just the chemo that was causing me to be sick. It was normal for us after all these years.

Tonight was a night that no one was scheduled to spend the night and I was glad. I needed time to think, to decompress from the last week and to figure out how much more fight I had in me. Sooner or later we were going to have to admit that treatments weren't working. Instead, they were killing me slower and there were decisions to be made. I could continue the platelet and blood transfusions and join an experimental trial or I could say enough and let this disease win.

I'd been sure just a few weeks ago but since meeting Wyatt, I was having a moment of crisis on the decision front. I didn't want him to change how I felt about illness and my fight to live. I didn't want anyone to have an affect on those choices but I had to admit that he had given me a reason to pause.

I knew I'd never be healthy like I wanted to be or even deserved to be. Then again, neither would Wyatt. I wasn't even sure that he felt the same about me. He could just want to remain friends and I'd have to be okay with that. He was my first true hospital friend in all of these years I'd spent here at OMMH.

I spent the evening watching him sleep on Facetime while I watched movies and read. I was tired but sleep just wouldn't come. I stayed up much later than normal, finally falling asleep around four a.m.

The nurses must have told my mother about my late night because she let me sleep in. I woke after they'd already set up my last treatment round. The poison was already flowing and my breakfast was cold. As soon as I opened my eyes my mother called down to food services to order hot cereal so I could have something on my stomach before the nausea took over. We'd been through this many times before and she knew that it was the only thing that would stay put throughout the day.

While we waited for it to be delivered, she helped me change my pajamas and brush my teeth. As she brushed my hair, large clumps of hair came out on the brush. Mom frowned at the hair and pulled it from the bristles and tossed it in the trash.

"Looks like you're getting a haircut whether you wanted it or not."

She was very matter of fact about it. This was much different than the first time I lost my hair. She'd cried and asked why this was happening to me. Hell, she'd cried so much that I didn't bother to cry myself.

Over the years, the hair became less important. It was just a part of this war I was fighting and not having hair during chemo made the throwing up a little easier. I definitely tried to find the bright side of the entire situation.

By lunch time, Wyatt was awake and feeling rough.

"Hey, welcome back to the land of the living," I joked.

"Hey." It was all he could manage.

"The first few days are always rough. I swear it gets easier."

"When? Because it sure doesn't feel like it's ever going to get easier."

"A few weeks," I shrugged. "It is always worse once it's over. Your body stops believing the poison is killing you and tries to kill you itself."

"That sounds fun." His grimace told me that he didn't mean a word of that sentence and I laughed.

"No one told you this would be a damn carnival, Wyatt. All that was promised was some puke and horrible side effects."

"Got all of that. And a few other things too."

I thought about what to say next because I wanted him to know that things would get better but I also didn't want to take away from the truth of what he was feeling.

"Ask the nurses for some mouth swabs if the sores start. They will help. I'll have Mom bring you some hard candy tomorrow. They're great for the days you can't eat. And here is my best tip. Are you ready?"

"Sure."

"Don't let the nurses talk you out of eating anything. If you're craving it, that means you want food and any food is good. Yes, broccoli is better for you than sloppy joes but sometimes you can keep the greasy shit down and not the healthy stuff. And don't be afraid to complain. If something hurts, you have every right to bitch about it and no one should stop you. Just don't unpack your bags in Complaint Town because that gets old quickly and you want the nurses to help you, not find you a burden."

"Thanks, November. For everything."

"No thanks needed. This is all new to you and I've been around Cancerville a long time. Your cancer just showed up in a different place than mine but we're still cancer buddies. Fuck," I glanced at my mom, waiting for her to scold me for the use of the "f" word but she simply shook her head and went pack to her book. "I know that sounded cheesy and even a little weird but let's just be honest with one another. We're friends because we both have this horrible disease waging a war inside of us and we have one of two choices. Fight or die. I'm not ready to die just yet. Are you?"

He shook his head no and sighed heavily. "How do you do it?"

"Stay so beautiful even now?" I teased him, trying to lighten the mood.

"Stay so positive?"

"I don't. I have my moments when I'm sad and I hate cancer and I hate that I'm sick and that I've missed out on my entire childhood. I hate not having friends. I hate that I'm dying slowly. But the truth is, I can't change a damn thing. I have no power in this other than fighting and so fight I do. I'll keep fighting until the time comes when I know it's time to stop. Right now, I still have a little trace of hope and that keeps me going."

"How? You've done this so many times. How in the Hell are you still fighting? I'm ready to throw in the towel right now and it's only been a few days."

"I felt that way too when it all started. The sickness only lasts so long and then you start to feel human again. Once you feel you feel human, you start to forget the bad days. That's the only way you're going to survive this. Don't let the bad days make the good days not count. This disease doesn't fight fair and it doesn't care one single bit about us. It's up to you to decide how you're going to live through this. You're either a victim or you're the one in control of your disease and your health. You need to decide that early on."

"You amaze me, November. You've got it all figured out while I lie here feeling sorry for myself."

"She has her moments where she feels sorry for herself too. Don't let her fool you," my mother chimed in.

I shot her a menacing glare and then burst into laughter at her feigned fear.

"She's right. We all struggle with this and it's not easy to be the cancer kid. You will get frustrated and you will hate this disease but you'll also learn just how tough you are and how much you can survive."

I wasn't used to being the one to give the pep talk but my Dad had given me plenty over the years and it seems I'd learned a lot from him. Helping Wyatt understand this illness and how to fight it felt good but I could only do so much to help. It was up to him how he fought and if he fought.

For now, it was enough to just give him some advice. He had no one, not even his parents and I'd been living this for so long now. Being there for Wyatt was something I intended on continuing for as long as he wanted me to.

As the day wore on, Wyatt and I moved on to safer and happier topics. We enthusiastically discussed which of the Kardashians were better. Wyatt's answer was wrong. He said "NONE."

I was team Kourtney, especially since she'd been entangled with Travis. We also talked about our favorite shows other than reality shows. We found that we both loved to watch reruns of The Big Bang Theory and talked for hours about Sheldon, Penny and the crew.

By the time dinner came, we'd figured out that we liked the same things on tv for the most part and vowed to watch tv over facetime over the weekend. We both picked at our burgers and fries we'd ordered for dinner. I think I ate more than Wyatt but that was to be expected since he was sicker than I was right now.

Wyatt seemed a little more open to eating his ice cream cup and I laughed at how he moaned in happiness with the first bite of his plain vanilla. I was luckier and got chocolate and it was delicious and soothing considering my throat hurt after all the talking.

I was happier in here with Wyatt around and I could only hope that I was making his time here happier as well. While we ate our ice cream he told me about his favorite junk foods. He was a traditionalist, going with Doritos and Dr. Pepper. I was far more daring with Takis and Coke Zero.

"How can you eat those things?" He was serious in his inability to understand why the spiciness of Takis made me so happy.

"They're delicious, what are you talking about? How can you not love them?"

"Because they make my tongue hurt and my lips numb. I'm sorry but that doesn't scream happy snack time to me."

"Well, you're very wrong Wyatt."

"You're crazy but cute so I guess I can forgive you for the Takis."

"Forgive me? Forgive ME? No, no, you're the one that needs forgiving. How dare you trash my favorite snack."

We both fell into a fit of laughter.

Wyatt was quickly becoming someone I didn't want to live without and that was a problem. I pushed those thoughts aside and enjoyed the evening with him.

The next day my dad arrived bright and early with breakfast for me and Wyatt.

"French toast delivery," he called out as he entered the room. "Got Wyatt some too. Let's get you all set and then I'll run his down to him.

"I'll take it," Valerie, the overnight nurse who was about to leave, offered. "I gotta get one last set of vitals on him anyway. And that way the kids can eat together."

Dad handed over the styrofoam box of breakfast to her as if she were a thief who was going to run off with Wyatt's french toast and I giggled at how serious he was.

He set about getting me ready for breakfast and I prayed that I'd be able to keep this down. The day after the last treatment was usually a rough day but it was tradition for Dad to bring in breakfast to try to tempt me to eat more than a few bites of anything.I always tried extra for him but to be fair it wasn't easy.

My iPad rang with a facetime call from Wyatt and I couldn't stop the smile that formed. Dad cast a sideway glance at me while I answered.

"Hey Mr. C, thanks for breakfast."

"Good Morning, Wyatt. I hope you're able to keep some of it down."

"I'm going to do my best," Wyatt replied. "Morning, Vem," he said using the nickname he knew I hated.

I smirked and said "Good morning."

"Wyatt," my dad chimed in. "How are you feeling?"

"Not so great, Mr. C. I had no idea I could throw up thic much and still be alive."

"Better get used to that," I added. "You'll be puking a lot in the coming days."

"God, I hope not. This must be what Hell is like."

Dad and I both laughed and I took a small bite of breakfast. Wyatt followed suit and made a face that I knew well. He wasn't going to keep the food down for long.

"Take your time," my dad advised him. "November used to throw up every time she ate when we first started chemo. Ask the nurses to get your oncologist to prescribe some anit-nausea medicine. It will help you keep food down. You need to eat to survive chemo."

"He's right," Valerie added as she came into view on the iPad from Wyatt's room. "Hey November, how you feeling today?"

"Hey Val, I'm okay. Tired but good I guess."

"Don't hesitate to call if you feel worse. I'll be in in a bit to get your vitals. Nice breakfast choice, Mr. Collins."

Dad waved at her, his mouth full of eggs. He was a big hit with the nurses here and I was thankful to have him around all the time. Dad made this time spent in the hospital bearable.

We spent the morning watching tv in between me napping. The first few days after chemotherapy meant I slept a lot trying to get over the week before. It was better than throwing up while on chemo though. Wyatt was going through Hell this week and he was all alone and that bothered me more than I let on.

I wished his parents understood how important support meant during this course of treatment and how lonely hospitals are. The nurses were doing their best to be present for him and I hated that I couldn't just go sit by his bed and hold his hand when he was sick. Cancer sucked and I hated it now more than ever.

Chapter Five

Wyatt's first chemo treatment was done and I was finally feeling well enough to be awake most of the day. We had spent every waking hour on Facetime and I was having trouble remembering a time before I'd met him. He'd become my best friend in such a short time.

I couldn't wait for the day that I could go to his room and actually sit next to him. I wasn't sure when that would be. This coming week would tell us whether the new course of treatments were working. If they weren't, there would be decisions that needed to be made and I wasn't sure that my parents would listen if I decided to not continue with treatment.

I had started to accept the fact that I was going to die sooner rather than later but my parents hadn't. They were convinced that the doctors would cure me. I hoped they were right but somewhere deep in my heart, I knew that they weren't even close to being right.

I did my best not to think about it but it was getting more and more difficult. My doctor was great and I loved her, but she was also honest with me. The chances that this course of treatment would be successful in stopping the cancer weren't good. I was a fighter, her words, but the opponent was strong and resilient.

My blood work needed to be damn near perfect for me to get a few months off. I wasn't going to get a chance to think much less figure out where to go from here if it wasn't. I'd have to make a decision quickly and get into an experimental treatment that wasn't guaranteed to even be successful but it may be my only shot at surviving this disease.

I was seventeen years old. I shouldn't be making life or death choices. I should be going to prom and deciding which college I wanted to attend after graduation. I should be dating boys like Wyatt who would try to get in my pants. Instead I was here, in a hospital bed, worried if I were going to live long enough to ever have sex.

My life had changed at eleven years old and there wasn't a damn thing anyone could do about it either. My grandma always said that 'God only gave the toughest battles to the strongest people' but I think she's full of shit. How the Hell did God know how strong I could be? It's not like He had answered any of my parents' prayers. The cancer had kept coming back no matter how many hours my mother spent in church lighting candles or how many prayer lists I'd been added to.

Cancer didn't seem to care that God thought I was strong. Cancer only wanted to kill me.

I hated cancer. I would always hate cancer. It was a filthy, disgusting disease that was running around inside of my body causing havoc. And it ruined my childhood.

I was still angry at cancer when Dr. Morales stopped in.

"How's my favorite patient feeling today?"

"I've had better days."

"Still feeling sick from the chemo?" She was instantly concerned and put the stethoscope to my chest to listen to my heart.

"No. Well yes, but it is more of a bad mental health day."

"Ah, cancer rage. Happens to the best of them, kiddo. When is your next visit with Toni?"

Toni was my therapist and I'd been seeing her since my diagnosis six years ago. My mother had insisted that I needed someone to talk to about my cancer. I hated to admit that she was right but having Toni in my life had been helpful. She'd helped me deal with a lot of emotions that I wouldn't have been able to process on my own.

"This week but I'm not in the mood to discuss anything with her right now."

"Understandable. I won't ask but before we drop it, don't be afraid to ask for help if you need it. Any of the nurses will be happy to sit and talk with you."

I sighed and nodded. Right now all I wanted was to be left alone to wallow in my self-pity.

Dr. Morales continued on with my exam, looking over my chart and bloodwork. "I hear you've made a friend here. I stopped in and checked on Wyatt for Dr. Kaopua this morning. He's cute."

"Dr. Morales!" I exclaimed, feigning shock. "He's way too young for you, isn't he?"

"November, be nice. I'm not that old."

"You're too old for a seventeen year old boy with cancer. Besides, you're my doctor. Stop trying to be friends with my friends."

We both laughed and she grew serious again. "It's good that you're able to help him. You of all people know how hard this can be and without support it's even harder. Just don't overextend yourself, okay."

She was right, of course. I knew all about being a cancer patient and how hard this was emotionally and physically. I'm glad that I could be there for Wyatt but right now, I could certainly use a friend of my own.

Not long after Dr. Morales left, my Facetime rang and Wyatt was there as soon as I hit accept.

"Hey, you okay?" I could hear the genuine concern in his voice.

I shrugged.

"Talk, November. What's going on?"

I was crying before I could stop the tears and Wyatt waited until I could speak.

"I'm just sick of cancer."

"I get that."

"I know you do but you're just starting. I've been doing this for six years. Treatments aren't working anymore."

"I haven't been at this as long as you but I do know it sucks. I don't want to do this again but here's the thing, November, we don't really have a choice. I don't want to die and I don't want you to die."

The sigh was long and sadness filled it.

"I may not get a choice in the matter."

"No, you may not, but are you willing to go down without a fight? Are you going to just let cancer get the best of you?"

"No."

"What was that? I didn't hear you." He leaned closer to the iPad and all I could see was his ear.

"NO."

"Good. That's the right attitude. We're gonna do this and we're gonna win together. We can ring that stupid bell at the same damn time."

"What if I never get to ring the bell?" My voice was a whisper and the fear was evident when I spoke.

"You can't think that way, November. You have to believe you're going to ring it. And I'll be right beside you."

"How are you so positive right now? I remember being so damn scared during my first week in the hospital. I was sure I was going to die from the vomiting and how bad my back felt after chemo."

"I'm all alone here. What choice do I have? If I don't believe that I'm going to beat this tumor, then I'm as good as dead."

"You're not alone."

"Thank you," he said, trying to hide his tears from me. It made him more human in my eyes and even more attractive than he already was.

"We're in the same boat, really. Only difference is I have my parents here all the time. But, I don't have any friends that show up. My sister barely makes an appearance lately."

"Maybe she's scared. I would be if it were my sister in here."

"Maybe. I miss her. She reminds me of home."

"I think seeing you here reminds her that you're not at home and that's hard to accept. Imagine how hard it must be for her knowing that you're here and your mom and dad are always here too. She's being left to raise herself for the most part."

I thought about it for a long while before I spoke again. "I hadn't really thought of it like that. It's been hard on Mom leaving Tracy at home all the time to be here. I've been selfish expecting her to be here every day."

"She would be here anyway. She's your mom and she loves you. I wish mine loved me the same way."

"I'm sure she does, Wyatt."

"No she doesn't. If she did, she would be here with me instead of drinking and hanging out on boats with rich people."

"I wish I could tell you why she's not here."

"It's not your problem."

"It's not yours either. You have to forgive her and move on. You've got me. I'm not going anywhere."

"You better not."

From there on, we lightened the conversation and watched movies together, arguing over if Die Hard was a Christmas movie or not. I knew that he was still upset but I fully understood the need to not discuss it anymore.

I wanted to make Wyatt forget being in the hospital for the night if that was possible. He'd had a rough few days and needed a break. I did too and it was nice to hear him laugh and argue with me over movies.

He had quickly become the best friend I'd ever had and I knew that I was falling in love with him. I was scared of that more than I was scared of dying. I had no idea if he felt the same way or even thought of me as more than some girl he'd met in the hospital.

We were just about to watch another movie when someone came bounding into his room.

"Wyatt, what the fuck is up?" The teenage boy was about our age and seemed to know Wyatt well. Our connection ended abruptly and I wondered who he was.

I didn't bother to try calling him back. He obviously didn't want his friend to meet me and I would respect that. It hurt but really, I wasn't someone he'd known long so why would he introduce me to his friends?

I closed my iPad and opened my History book to study. I had to pass this class in order to graduate on time and I was determined to do just that especially since my guidance counselor had advised me to quit and focus on getting better.

Obviously that counselor didn't know me at all. I wasn't a quitter. I would graduate with my class even though 99% of them had never laid eyes on me. I hadn't stepped inside of a school in years, instead working with a homebound teacher or my mother to pass the classes I needed to.

I did my best not to think about Wyatt and his friend, even when I heard their laughter from down the hall. I got up and slammed my door shut, angry that he'd just dismissed me the way he did. Part of me thought I had no right to be pissed, the other part, the part I was listening to, said he was being a dick and I was allowed to be angry at him.

I went with that part. As the night wore on, I chose to ignore his facetime calls after the laughter stopped from down the hall. I wanted to hate him that night because he'd hurt me and I didn't even understand it at the time

So I ignored him. He called over and over and even had a nurse check on me for him. I still refused to answer his calls. I needed him to feel bad and I wanted him to be hurt like I was. I didn't want to hear his excuses or his reasons for what he'd done.

I did my best to focus on my history lesson and turned my iPad off. He would have to get the message one way or another. It wasn't my problem to deal with anymore tonight.

I studied until midnight, then turned off the lights, turned over and went to sleep. The next morning dawned with me waking up and immediately puking all over the bed and floor. I hit the call button for the nurse and sat on the edge of the bed, shivering and nauseous.

I knew immediately that this was more than just a late reaction to the chemo. Something was wrong and I was sick. This wasn't a good sign and I knew it.

I was puking again by the time the nurses hit the room. They came running after hearing my retching over the call box. Valerie and Pam grabbed me up off the bed and onto a chair, holding a pan in front of me while Toni and Tricia pulled sheets and blankets from my bed. They moved quickly so that they could get me back in the bed as fast as possible.

I held onto my puke pan like my life depended on it and Valerie never left my side. Tricia was calling housekeeping but already mopping up vomit as she did. As soon as the bed was changed, I was helped into new pjs and put back into the bed.

My temperature was 103 and I couldn't keep anything down, having vomited another three times since the nurses' arrival. I begged for more blankets but Valerie refused. I knew that I wasn't allowed more until the fever was down but at that moment, I didn't care about rules. I was cold.

This had hit me out of nowhere. I'd been just fine the night before. I know the nurses were worried and had already placed calls to Dr. Morales and my parents. My mother would be terrified and was most likely driving like a mad woman through town right now. She would be freaking out and I hated that I was putting her through this.

Valerie was trying her best to get me to drink something while Toni hooked up an IV bag of fluids when my mother came running in.

"November, are you okay? What's wrong?"

I collapsed into her hug and cried. She held me until I'd cried myself to sleep. I slept for six hours before I woke up to puke all over the place again. After being cleaned up again, mom helped me back to bed.

"Dr. Morales will be in soon. In the meantime, let's get some gatorade or pedialyte in you."

I groaned at the thought of either but lifted my heavy head when she held out the bottle and straw to me. I took a sip and instantly gagged.

"I can't," I complained, laying back down.

Mom shook her head and helped lift my head again for another sip. "You have to stay hydrated, November Rain."

"Okay," I groaned and took another sip. I let her help me lay back down and fell asleep instantly. This illness, whatever it was, was spreading fast through my system.

I woke just as Dr. Morales came into the room.

"How are you feeling?" She already had my chart pulled up on her iPad and was looking over blood work results.

"Like I'm dying."

"Well then, it's a good thing you're here in the hospital already." She winked at me and smiled over at my mother. "I promise you that you're not dying. You have the flu so I'm going to isolate you for the next few days. Sorry, Mom, that means you have to go home. Only ones allowed in are the nurses and me. From here on out full isolation gear when we come in. With your white count so low right now, we just can't take any chances."

Mom frowned and started to argue, but thought twice about it and began to gather her things.

"How long is this for, Dr.?" Her concern was evident but she did her best to remain calm.

"Hopefully just a few days, but it all depends on how well she's feeling and what her counts are."

My mother nodded and leaned over to kiss my forehead and tell me that she was just a facetime call away. I hugged her tightly, not wanting her to leave.

"Can't she stay?" I wasn't above begging.

"No, I'm sorry, she can't. We need you in complete isolation so as not to risk any complications. With Mom having been around others, we just can't take the risk."

I let my tears fall and did my best to let go of my mother. She held on just as tightly and stayed until Dr. Morales forced her out of my room.

I could hear them talking out in the hall but I couldn't make out what they were discussing. Knowing my mother, she was demanding to be allowed to sleep just outside the door. Most days I wanted my independence from her but when I was this sick, I wanted my mommy with me, to take care of me and keep me from falling apart.

But now, I was alone, in isolation and not allowed any visitors. I understood that it was so I could get better but I didn't like it at all. I lay there in my bed and stared at the ceiling, feeling sorry for myself. I ignored my facetime calls and cried for the better part of the day.

Somewhere deep inside I understood this feeling of despair was because I was sick and that it wasn't who I really was. I rarely became this emotional but this illness caught me off guard and I wasn't ready to deal with any of it. I had been prepared to be done with chemo and just coast through the few weeks until I could go home and back to a normal life. Or as normal of a life as I had.

I wanted to be in my own bed, in my own room, where I didn't have to deal with nurses or IVs or Wyatt. I wasn't even sure that he cared that I wasn't answering his calls. Had a nurse told him I was sick?

It was the last thought I had before drifting to sleep finally. I barely woke when Valerie entered the room with a new CNA. She introduced her as Brooklyn and I opened my eyes long enough to make eye contact. They set up a new bag of fluids and added in some flu medication. I didn't bother to listen to what it was. I just wanted to sleep without interruption.

Valerie tucked me in and took my vitals before she left the room. I appreciated all of my nurses but right now I didn't want to see any of them. I slept restlessly for the next seven hours, only opening my eyes when a nurse or phlebotomy entered the room.

Dr. Morales had me on a bland diet featuring chicken broth and I struggled to get any of it down. Once I had managed to eat some of it, it all came right back up. I didn't see the point of trying to eat it after that.

My fever lingered and I shivered more and more. I was allowed one sheet and thin blanket so I was convinced I was going to freeze to death. Intellectually I knew better but in my fevered mind I was certain it was going to happen.

I finally woke late in the night and turned on the tv just to fill the silence of the room. The IV bag had been replaced sometime while I slept and there was a tray of food sitting on the counter just in case I woke up to eat. I had no appetite and therefore no desire to see what was on the tray.

The light from the tv filled the room with color from time to time and I would focus on the show that was playing. It was some older comedy show from the sixties and I didn't get most of the jokes that had the live audience laughing loudly. I didn't care that it made no sense to me, I just wanted to not hear the silence now.

I propped my bed up so I could be in a seated position and moved the pillows around until I was finally comfortable. Looking at the clock, it said three a.m. The light from the parking lot below snuck in between the slats of the blinds and I wondered what the people in the world around me were doing now. Was anyone other than me and the nurses who worked overnights awake?

Would anyone want to be awake at this time of morning? Was my mother home sleeping? Or was she awake worrying about me? I wanted to facetime her right now and tell her how much I loved and missed her but I decided to wait til it was a better time. I didn't want to risk waking her up.

She'd been through a lot as my mother and deserved her rest. I couldn't imagine how hard my cancer had been for her. I didn't have children so I didn't know what it felt like to know that your daughter may die at a very young age.

I thought back over all the times I'd been in the hospital and how she'd always been there with me. She stayed every single day, only going home because Tracy needed her too. I worried that she hadn't been there enough for Tracy and that it was going to come back to haunt them when I was gone.

Tracy seemed to be well adjusted and popular but I truly didn't get to spend much time with her anymore. We had never been particularly close growing up but I did love my sister enough to know that I didn't want her to be hurt because she just happened to have a sister with cancer.

Unfortunately, in the end, I was going to hurt them all. I was going to die much younger than anyone had expected when I was born. It was just the way it was. We all had to come to terms with that.

I tried my damnedest to stop this line of thinking but it was the middle of the night and I was sick and my brain just didn't care that these thoughts were hurting me. I couldn't turn my brain off and it led me down a very sad place that ended with me crying into my pillow until the sun came up.

Chapter Six

By the fourth day the puking had finally stopped. I still felt horrible but a little more human than before. I hadn't spoken to Wyatt at all. My father had called him and let him know that I was sick. I wanted to yell at my dad for that but I thought better of it. He'd tried to be a good father so I'd forgive him for not knowing that I was still mad at Wyatt.

Mom dominated the calls, asking about my blood counts and how I was feeling. She'd been in constant contact with my nurses and Dr. Morales so I felt it was redundant to go through it all again but she insisted.

I was still on fluids and medication but at least I wasn't throwing up any longer. My throat was raw and my body ached all over but I was alive and that counted at this point. Dr. Morales had reassured me that I needed just a few more days of rest and then we could discuss what my counts were for my leukemia.

I was worried that I wouldn't get good news but hoped for the best clinical trial possible if that were the case. I'd done some research before this last round of chemo and there were some good ones out there. Many of them had horrible side effects but if it meant I stayed alive, it would be worth it.

I rested most of the day, still thinking about where I would go if this round of chemo had failed. A bone marrow transplant was always an option but I didn't want Tracy to have to go through that if possible. She was scared and I didn't blame her. Being my sister was hard enough. I had no plans to involve Tracy in my cancer unless I had no other choice.

My mother on the other hand had every intention of forcing Tracy to be tested to see if she was a match. Typically a sibling was the best match possible for bone marrow. I tried to explain to mom the reasons why I didn't want to involve Tracy but she didn't listen. She insisted that my sister would want to do this for me. I didn't agree or even believe that. Tracy and I had never been close. She didn't understand my illness and I didn't understand her life. She was envious of the attention my parents showered on me and I was jealous of how she got to make her own decisions and live her life while I was stuck in a perpetual state of waiting to live.

Tracy dated. I'd never even had a boy have a crush on me because I was never in school long enough to even make a friend muchless find a boy to like me. Tracy had friends, lots of them, and they loved her. Tracy went to the movies and to the fair. She went to school dances and was on the volleyball team. I was in the hospital.

Part of me hated her because she didn't have cancer. The rest of me was thrilled she'd never have to live this type of life. I wanted her to be a teenager and have all of the experiences that I couldn't. Her life shouldn't change because her sister was dying.

I wanted to live the life she had. I'd have given almost anything for that life. Except my life wasn't that way. My life involved bloodwork and hospital stays, isolation and no friends, worry and fear. I spent most of my time in the hospital and when I was home, I was sick and not able to go out. My friends were all adults, except for Wyatt and I wasn't even sure that I could still count him as a friend. I hadn't spoken to him in days. Most of that was my fault but he owned some of that as well. I also wasn't sure that I wanted him as a friend right now. I was still hurt and angry with him. That hadn't ended because I'd gotten sick. If anything, it had made me even angrier. I'd been so out of it that I had no idea if he had even tried to contact me.

Wyatt was the last thought I had before I fell asleep for a long nap. My body was still healing from the chemo and the flu. My dreams were filled with him and I woke up wanting nothing more than to speak to him.

I picked up my iPad and hit the Facetime button, hoping he wasn't pissed at me and would actually answer my call. It rang until it disconnected and my heart sank. He was pissed and I didn't blame him. I hadn't been a very good friend at all to him. I'd known he needed someone to be there during his first round of chemo but I hadn't been. It didn't matter why. What mattered was that my only friend in years had needed me and I'd been too self-absorbed to care.

I sank back into my bed and sighed. I'd let him down. Hell, I'd let myself down as well.

A few moments later I nearly jumped out of my skin when my Facetime rang and scared me. I saw his name and my face lit up into the biggest smile. I tried my best to act natural when I answered.

"Hey, stranger. How ya feeling?"

I sounded stupid and silently kicked myself for sounding like an idiot but it was too late now. The words were out of my mouth and I was sure he'd laugh at me.

"Hey, I heard you had a rough week. You feeling better?"

"I guess. I'm not puking anymore and the fever is gone, so that's good. Dr. Morales will be in later. How did the chemo go?"

"It was Hell. You were 1000% right about that. I didn't know that I could puke without having food in my body for days on end but it didn't stop. Did you know that stomach acid is a bright green?"

I laughed a little. "You know, I did."

His laughter mixed with mine and I knew in that moment that we were okay. I hadn't lost my friend and that made everything okay.

"Hey, Wyatt."

"Yeah?"

"I'm sorry I wasn't around when you were going through all of that. It sucks to go through it alone."

My apology was sincere and I meant every word. I really was sorry.

"No big deal, November. You were going through your own crap. Do you always get so sick after chemo?"

"No, this was a first."

"Was it the chemo or something else?"

"The flu. Cancer couldn't get to me so he called in a friend to blindside me."

Wyatt shook his head and looked concerned. "Are you okay now?"

I shrugged. "Honestly?"

"Of course. If you can't be honest with your cancer buddy, who can you be honest with?"

"I don't know. This threw a wrench into things because I should have known by now if this last round of chemo had helped. But because I got sick, the bloodwork was all messed up so I won't know until Dr. Morales orders all the tests again."

"What happens after that?"

"Well, I'll have to make a decision on whether or not I want to get into a clinical trial if the chemo didn't kill the cancer this time."

"And if you don't do a trial? What happens?"

"I go home to die. They'll make me as comfortable as possible while the cancer takes over my body and eventually kills me."

"How long?"

"Could be days. Could be years. No one really knows. All I know is that my cancer is more aggressive than ever and it was rapidly spreading before this round of chemo."

He sat silently for a while, both of us scared that death was too close for comfort for either of us. Time passed slowly and neither of us spoke for a long time, each lost in thought.

"November," he spoke quietly. "It's okay to be scared. I'm scared too."

"Thanks," I said just as quietly.

I was scared. I was absolutely terrified of dying. Ever since I'd met Wyatt, I wanted to live more than ever.

"Hey, wanna watch The Avengers?" He interrupted my thoughts and I was so grateful for the distraction.

"Again? How many times can we watch that movie?"

"500 times seems like a good amount," he said laughing as we both logged in and pulled the movie up so we could spend the evening watching it together over Facetime.

I wasn't a fan of superhero movies but Wyatt had forced me to watch this movie so many times since we'd met that I could quote most of it as we watched. I'd grown to love it because Wyatt did. I gasped at all the right places and cheered along with Wyatt at the right times.

For two hours, I forgot that I was dying and focused on how The Avengers saved the world. Maybe I'd get a superhero of my own to save me.

Those two hours were the best two hours I'd had in the hospital in my entire life. We laughed and joked about how Marvel always made their superheroes a little quirky and how much fun we had watching them. Before Wyatt, I hadn't watched a movie with a friend. Not ever.

I was glad to have him here to help me pass the time and to make this place a little more bearable. I don't know how I'd survived all this time without him. I was so glad that he wasn't mad at me.

I had my friend back and I wasn't going to let him go this time. No matter what it took, I'd be there for him in and out of the hospital. Spending this time with him watching movies really had helped me keep my mind off of Dr. Morales and test results. Tomorrow was another day and I could deal with all of that then. Today was a day I got to be a teenage girl, hanging out with a boy that she liked, even if it was in a hospital over Facetime.

That day went by so fast and we fell asleep still connected. I even think I fell asleep with a smile on my face. The next morning I learned that my isolation restriction had been lifted and my mother and father could return. It had been weird without them here for so long but honestly, it had made me even more thankful that they showed up and that they cared so much about me and my health.

I was one of the lucky kids in here. My parents cared enough to show up and be here to help me through my illness. I knew it was rare. I'd seen it so many times, and now, with Wyatt, it really hit home how lucky I was. I couldn't imagine having to face cancer alone. I was pretty darn sure that I wasn't strong enough to do so. I needed my mom and dad to be here so that I didn't dwell on the fact that I was so sick. They helped me in so many ways, from school, to giving me emotional support and for never making me feel like I couldn't survive this disease.

At the end of the day, I knew that they'd have my back and fight for me to get the best care here and everywhere. They wouldn't let me give up because they knew I could do this and that nothing would stop me if I put my mind to it.

I wished that every kid facing cancer or any disease were lucky enough to have parents like mine but the reality was that mine were special and I made a note to thank them as soon as they arrived.

Mom would be so happy to be back. She thrived when she had me to take care of. Of course, there was so much else she should be doing with her life besides spending it inside this room with me, but she never made me feel like she was giving up anything to be here. Dad was exactly the same way. He showed up nightly with a smile and a hug. I loved them, more than I'd ever told them.

I wondered what it was really like for Wyatt, not having his family here to support him. Did they call him? He never spoke about them and it worried me that he was alone in this fight.

Except he wasn't truly alone. He had me and my parents. We cared about him and wanted the best for him. That should be enough right? I knew it wasn't. Nothing was a substitute for your own family but we would still be there for him when he needed us. That's just who we were.

I was dressed for the day and eating toast when Mom arrived with her bag of knitting and crosswords. She kissed my cheek and settled in as if she'd never been gone. A few minutes passed of her getting settled before she started filling me in on all the neighborhood gossip.

Seems that Alexandra and Nicole had had a falling out over a tree that Alex said was too ugly to stay and Nicole yelled obscenities over the fence about Alex's dog always barking and keeping her up.

They were best friends who had lived beside one another for ten years but every once in a while, something set them off and they didn't speak for weeks. Then one day, everything went back to normal.

Mom said this one was brought on by the fact that Nicole had gotten a job offer in another state and Alex was upset that she may actually take it. I laughed but felt bad for them. Friendships were important but so was supporting your friend when they got new opportunities.

She moved on to telling me about Tricia and her mother Pam. Seems they'd won some money on the lottery and had plans to travel once they cashed it all in. Tricia and Pam were dear friends of my mother and they'd asked her to take a cruise with them next summer. I really hoped my mom would go. She deserved a vacation.

Angela, one of the new neighbors, had recently had a baby and Tracy was babysitting for her. Mom said that Tracy didn't really like babies so she wasn't sure why she'd taken the job but it gave her freedom and money so she didn't question her insanity.

I, on the other hand, did question it. What was my sister thinking? Who wanted to change diapers and listen to crying babies for hours? I certainly never had any need to be around babies. Hell I didn't even want to go to the floor that the babies were on here at the hospital.

I half listened to Mom continue on with her gossip and half paid attention to the news on the tv simply because it wasn't about babies.

By the time I was done with breakfast, they'd come in to take more blood. Seems Dr. Morales wanted a complete work up so she knew where we stood. I would have answers tomorrow and know what my next step would need to be.

I needed to know that next step so I could start to plan the rest of my life. Either I was in remission or I was looking at clinical trials. The choices weren't great but I'd narrowed down a few that seemed like they were promising. I just needed Dr. Morales's input on them before I could make a true decision. I hoped I wouldn't need that input but somewhere deep inside I knew I would.

Cancer had been a tougher opponent than I'd thought it would be. Six years of fighting and I wasn't any healthier. In fact, I might actually be sicker than when I'd started. Chemo was rough on the body and it had given mine a run for its money in more ways than one.

By the time Mom was done filling me in on the gossip, I was ready to crawl out of my brain because she'd talked for well over an hour. Good thing I was still in my "I appreciate my mom" stage or I'd have begged her to be quiet.

I let her talk as long as she wanted, about things I didn't want to know about. It had been too long since I'd seen her or had the chance to listen to her talk. I just kinda needed my mom's voice to fill the room.

When she was done talking about the neighbors she asked about Wyatt. I filled her in on how he'd been doing and she let it slip that dad had been by to visit him when he'd stopped in to peek in on me. She said that Dad wanted to let Wyatt know that he wasn't alone in this, even with me being sick and not able to be there for him. I smiled at her because I knew that she'd had a hand in that and I was grateful to her for it.

Wyatt had become important to me and my parents had seen it and acted on it. How could I not be thankful that they were my parents and loved me enough to care about someone I cared about. I was lucky and I knew it.

We spent the day playing games and laughing at tv shows. It felt good to have her here with me. I hadn't realized how much I'd missed her. I thought about how many kids were alone in their hospital rooms, hooked up to machines that they didn't understand, fighting illnesses that they may never survive and that didn't care about them. I thought about how many of those kids only had the nurses in here for company and only when they had a moment of free time to spend with them. Most of these kids were alone every day and that broke my heart.

One of those kids was my friend and I knew firsthand how hard it was for him to have no one there at his side through this. I wished with all I had that I could change that for all of them and that I could somehow convince their families to see how much they needed them.

Mom had told me years ago that not every family had the opportunity to be here every day like she was. She'd explained how a lot of families were single parent families with other children they had to take care of and that made it impossible for them to sit in the hospital every day with their child even though it was exactly where they wanted to be.

I hadn't understood it then and I still didn't understand it now. There was no way I'd ever let my child be in the hospital alone. There was no way I'd ever let my child feel like they were alone in their fight.

That got me thinking about having children and how that wasn't a likelihood for me ever. I'd never get married or have a family. I probably wouldn't even be here to see my sister graduate from high school and that bothered me. A lot.

I didn't want to die. I think I've said that before but I really meant it now. Staying alive was not an option or a desire, it was a must and I intended to fight as hard as I could.

"Maybe we can figure out how to help Wyatt out once you're out of here, November."

I shook the thoughts from my head and focused on my mother once again.

"I think that would be nice, Mom. He's turning out to be a good friend."

"It's nice to see you make a friend, honey. It has been a long time since you've had someone your own age to hang out with and talk to. Maybe Wyatt would like to come stay for a little while this summer. We can plan some trips to the pool and the movies. Whatever you two want to do."

"Slow down, Mom. We're not dating and we're just friends."

"I wasn't suggesting," she said, shrugging her shoulders.

"Sure. I can see your mind working and I am your daughter. I know you, Mom. Can we just enjoy the fact that I have a friend and not focus on the part where he is a boy and I'm a girl? I don't want a boyfriend. I don't want you to try to marry off your dying daughter either. I understood long ago how my life would be."

"Oh, November, honey, you're not going to die alone. You're going to be just fine. We will fight this as long as we need to. There will be plenty of time for you to find someone to love and marry."

"We both know that isn't in the cards for me, Mom. We've both known that since I was eleven. It is okay to say that I'm dying. You're going to have to accept it sooner than later. I don't want you to be sad or caught off guard when it happens. I don't want you to cry, Mom."

"Honey, can we please not talk about this kind of thing? You're not going to die any time soon."

I could tell she was scared to admit it to herself. She was not prepared for me to die and probably never would be. I worried about my mother once I was gone. I prayed that Tracy would be her saving grace, that she'd continue on because of my sister. I had very little hope that this was the case though. She loved Tracy just as much as she loved me but Tracy didn't need her the way that I did and so my mom had spent all of her energy on keeping me alive all these years. Where would that energy go once I was gone?

Would she turn all of her attention on my sister? Or would my dad have to be the one that kept her busy? Would my mother survive my death with her sanity? It all remained to be seen but it wasn't something I had the luxury of focusing on right now.

Instead I had to figure out how to keep my beloved mother from marrying me off to Wyatt or some other boy as soon as she legally could. She meant well but she wasn't doing me any favors by trying to guilt some sick boy into being my boyfriend. Hell, I didn't even know if I wanted a boyfriend for that matter.

I'd once thought maybe I liked girls but that was just a passing phase when I was head over heels crushing on Megan Fox in my early teenage years. Now, I crushed more on her boyfriend, Machine Gun Kelly than I did her so I guess that made me straight with bi tendencies.

Anyway, I didn't really like labels so I turned that train of thought off. How had I even gotten there?

I realized it had been a long time since I'd spoken and my mother was staring at me as if she were waiting for me to say something.

"What?," I asked.

"You seemed like you got lost in thought for a bit. Wanna tell me what you were thinking about? "

"Megan Fox and Machine Gun Kelly."

"Who?" She asked innocently, like a mother who had no idea who the popular celebrities of the day were.

"A couple of actors. Oh and he sings too. Or raps. Or both, I guess. I don't know, Mom. I was just wondering how you went from Wyatt and I being friends to marrying me off to him."

"Honey, I don't want to marry you off. But I do want you to experience everything that life has to offer, including love."

"Love? You think that love will cure my cancer?"
"No. I think the doctors will cure your cancer but love will help you want to fight to live. So love is worth everything."

"Mom, I'm fighting. I'm fighting as hard as I can. I'm fighting for my life, for the breath in my body and I'm fighting because of you. I can't fight any harder than I am right now. And I don't need the stress of you trying to fix me up with a boy right now. I need to focus on school and getting better before I even consider wanting to decide if I want a boyfriend or not."

"I really hate when you do this, November. You're a teenage girl. You should be wanting to date boys and go to the Prom."

"I've never been a normal kid and I never will be. This is the hand that I was dealt by life and I have to play it out until I have no moves left and then I have to cheat."

My mom studied me for a bit before she spoke. "It's a shitty hand to be dealt, don't you think?"

"Yeah, but what choice do I have?"

"You've been strong for a really long time, November. I know you're tired. I know that you want to give up sometimes but I'm so glad that you're still here. You have so much left to do in this world."

I took the hand my mother offered me and held it tightly. I wanted to tell her that she was the reason that I fought so hard. I wanted her to know that without her here, I'd have given up a long time ago. I never wanted to be the reason she cried. I didn't want to hurt my mother any more than my mother wanted her child to die.

I was thankful that we were interrupted by Wyatt appearing in the doorway. He stayed just outside so that I didn't give him any germs and he didn't give me any. We had to be careful of course with each of us having just finished chemo.

"Hey Mrs. C, good to see you."

"Good Morning, Wyatt. How are you feeling today?"

"I'm good. Tired and a few unexpected side effects that I wasn't prepared for but, hey, I'm tough like November here."

I laughed and smiled over at him. "Tough huh? Just wait, you have no idea what's coming."

He ran a hand through his thick hair and nodded. "I have no doubt I'm about to find out. How are you doing today, Vem?"

"Vem? Who the hell is Vem?"

He shrugged and laughed. "I don't know, just something I figured I could call you. Easier than November, I guess."

"Don't. Please."

He nodded. "Got it. But you didn't answer me. How are you feeling?"

"Better for sure. A little tired but I'm really glad to be out of isolation and to have my mom back here with me."

"I bet she's even happier to be back."

We spent the next few minutes catching up before the nurses realized he was there and reigned us in. They forced Wyatt into a wheelchair and took him back to his room with him waving over his shoulder and his laughter filling the entire hallway as they did so.

I heard him calling out hellos to the other kids in the rooms between us and them laughing and yelling back to him. He was like a breath of fresh air on this unit and seemed to be loved by all the patients, not just me.

I wondered why the Universe sent him here. Was he meant to help me choose to fight or was he here just to be my friend when I needed one the most? Funny how he'd just shown up at the right time. I guess the Universe knew what it was doing and doing it in its own time for sure.

"You okay, honey?"

My mom's quiet question brought me back to reality and I nodded. I didn't need her analyzing my thoughts so I kept them to myself and lied.

"Yep. I was wondering what was for lunch."

She snatched the menu from the bedside tray and laughed. "Well let's have a look. Options are grilled cheese, chicken salad, chef salad or burger. What would you like?"

"I'll have the burger with fries, an orange, ice cream and a coke."

I listened as Mom called down my order and ordered her own lunch. It was nice to not have to eat alone again and I anxiously awaited having lunch with my mother.

Chapter Seven

Doctor Morales blew into my room the next morning like a hurricane about to destroy everything in her path. She held my paper chart in her hand and pulled it up on the computer the nurse drug in behind her. She flipped through her handwritten notes and jotted a few more down before she even said Good Morning.

The concern on her face was enough to make me worry but I held my breath and waited for her to speak.

"Your platelets are extremely low so I'm going to order a transfusion as soon as we can find a match. The leukemia hasn't changed at all with this course of chemotherapy. We need to start looking at clinical trials. I'm going to have my nurse send over several choices that I've been looking at for you. We need to make a decision quickly as several of the trials are about to close and if you want in to one, we need to get you presented as soon as possible. There is a chance they will reject you based on your counts but I'll fight for you and so will my team."

"Please slow down," I interrupted. "I need a minute to process this all."

"November, I know this isn't what you wanted or what we'd hoped for but we simply must act fast if you want to get into a trial. If you wait, you may not be able to get into one later."

She looked from me to my mother and I knew she was silently instructing my mom to help me move fast with my decision. But I needed a few moments to let it sink in.

"I know that Dr. Morales. You've made that clear. What I don't know right now is how I feel about any of this because I haven't had five minutes to let it all sink in and let my brain catch up to my feelings."

She rested her hand on my arm and squeezed. I knew beyond a shadow of a doubt that this wasn't what she'd hoped for. I also knew that she'd never have wanted to bring this news in here if she didn't have to. But....

She had. She'd vocalized my worst fears and here she was giving me moro seconds to decide the fate of my future. I wasn't ready to make that decision. If I made it now, I'd be dead. I needed to see the trials she suggested and see if any matched the ones I'd picked out. That was where I needed to start and I needed Dr. Morales to let me start there.

I looked between her and my mother and shook my head. "Don't try it. I said I need a few minutes to deal with this all. You can either give it to me, or I'll choose to do nothing and we'll all lose. Please get me those trials as soon as you can so I can look them over."

WIth that I dismissed her. My mother stepped out of the room with her and it didn't escape me that they were talking about my life and future without considering my wishes.

I didn't care at that moment. I was replaying everything Dr. Morales had said. I heard them over and over until it was all I could focus on.

The chemotherapy hadn't worked. I wasn't in remission. My cancer was stronger than the drugs now and that meant that I was going to die.

It was then that the anger grabbed hold of me and I lost it. I screamed loudly and threw the first thing I could get my hands on. The vase holding flowers sent by my mothers church shattered against the wall and sprayed out around the room. I collapsed into a ball of tears and screamed some more.

I was pissed off at everyone but mostly at this God my mother kept praying to. Why would he let this happen to me? Why was I going to die? Hadn't my mother prayed enough? She'd given an offering every week of her life and she was a good person.

I was a good person.

I didn't want to die.

I refused to die.

I wasn't about to let some imaginary man in the sky decide when it was time for my life to end. Fuck him. Fuck her. Fuck whatever they were.

Why?

Why?

Why me?

Why now?

Why couldn't my life have been normal? Why was I 'so strong' and given this disease? Why was I chosen? Why me? Why not Tracy? Or my mom? Or dad? Or anyone else? I'd never done anything wrong or hurt anyone at all. I was ELEVEN YEARS OLD FOR FUCKS SAKE when I got sick. I was a whore or a bad kid and I'd never been ungrateful. I'd never stolen anything or skipped a class or anything at all that deserved this.

I was so angry. I hated everyone at that point in time. And I had every right to feel it all.

I was so mad that I didn't even stop to think for a minute that I was going to fight. I just wanted and needed to feel this anger so that I could move past it.

I continued to scream when the nurses came running in and then left quietly. I continued to scream when my mother shut the door to my room. I threw things and I kicked my feet and screamed even louder. All the while tears fell down my face unchecked and I was exhausting myself.

Soon I'd scream and cry myself to sleep and to be fair, I probably needed that to happen so that I'd shut up. I was getting on my own damn nerves by this point.

I woke up several hours later, twisted up in the blankets, to find my mother seated at my bedside, watching me sleep. As soon as she saw I was awake, she pulled me into her arms and held me close.

"Shhh, honey. Now is not the time to talk. I need you to listen to me."

Every fiber of my being did not want to do that but what choice did I have? So, I listened while I let her hold me.

"Whatever you decide, I'm behind you. I don't want you to do anything you don't want to." Her voice shook with hesitation and fear but she continued to speak. "This is your life and your illness and you have to make the choice that is right for you. You've fought this for so many years and I don't blame you if you're tired of fighting. I can sit here and tell you that I don't want you to die and beg you to make the decision I feel is right for you but what I've come to realize is that I've already asked so much of you for most of your life. Now is when I need to understand that you're almost a grown woman and that you can make your own choices. Before you make that choice though, please think about the people who love you, November. Think about how much it will hurt your father and I. How much it will hurt Tracy to not have her big sister to help her as she grows up. Think about how much Wyatt will miss you and how much he will miss out on if you're gone. But most of all, my sweet baby girl, think about how much you will miss if you aren't here. I love you so much November Rain. You are my firstborn, the daughter who made me a mother and you are the first completely true love of my life. I don't want you to die. I don't want to have to say goodbye to you. It's not right. It's just not right."

By this point my mother was sobbing and her words were no longer making sense. I clung to her as if she were my life line to this world. I couldn't let go. Her words reverberated in my head, her pleas, her desperation echoing amongst my own thoughts and they started to all jumble together and nothing made sense anymore. I didn't know what words were her's and what were mine. All I knew is that right here and right now, I needed my mommy and she was here, holding me and saying she loved me. She promised she'd let me go if it was what I wanted but at what cost? Would it destroy her if I was gone?

Could I take that chance?

Chapter Eight

My mother was true to her word. She gave me time to think and make my own decision without interference. She kept my father and sister away from the hospital that night and the next day.

Mom and Dr. Morales had left me with all of the information that I would need to make a decision and they gave me the space to make it. Any questions I had I wrote down and emailed to Dr. Morales and Mom. They were answered in a timely fashion with truth and no bias. I was grateful for that because it was what I needed. Making this decision wasn't easy, but as my mother liked to say so often, nothing worth having was easy.

I sat in my bed, surrounded by files and papers spread everywhere, in complete silence. My thoughts ran the gamut of wanting to just let it all go, and fighting. I was no closer to a decision about this than I was about what I wanted to be if I were to grow up.

All of the case studies blurred together and I was more confused than ever. I'd read over the top four clinical trials that Dr. Morales had chosen along with two that I'd chosen. We were on the same page with three of the trials so I tried my best to focus on those.

My number one choice was her second choice. I read through the side effects once more and frowned.

Possible side effects and side effects seen in 1 out of 4 patients include uncontrollable vomiting, debilitating migraines, rash and redness over ¾ of the body, and diarrhea. This trail is currently in Phase II or the stage of investigating if the trial drug is working. We are currently accepting applications for this trial with a maximum number of 50 (fifty) participants who will work with our doctors as well as their own physician(s). Primary point of contact will be the patient's primary physician. There is no compensation for this trial and most insurance plans will not cover the cost. Patient or patient's guardians, if a minor, will incur the expense which can be broken down into payments. See financial information for details. Deadline is June 24th with final selections confirmed July 1st. Patient must be available to begin the trial immediately upon selection.

During the trial period of one year, patients will remain hospitalized for a period of three (3) months, with discharge after for a period of two (2) months, returning to hospital for the remaining seven (7) months to ensure that all trial successes or failures are recorded in real time. Patients must meet minimum age requirements and must currently be out of traditional options for treatment. During this time period, the patient will refrain from any other treatments including chemotherapy and/or radiation. Patient willingly submits to having blood samples drawn daily to continue to monitor the effect the drug is having on the patient's white blood cells. Patient will also consent to a bone marrow draw to determine if the drug is having any effect.

Along with physician statements and all charts pertaining to the patient's treatment, the patient must submit in writing why this trial was chosen.

Patient and the patient's physician understand that should the patient be removed from this trial, a minimum period of six months is required before the patient would be eligible for chemotherapy treatment again. Patient understands that there is no guarantee of a cure or of survival if removed from the program or otherwise.

This is a clinical trial of a new drug currently being tested to treat specific types of leukemia including AML. There is limited data available on the viability of this drug at this time. The makers of this drug and the physicians and researchers involved are not liable should the patient not survive the trial.

I tossed the page back into the pile. None of that helped make my decision any easier. I had no idea why I'd chosen that trial other than it seemed the least invasive and was in a good stage that could show results given the preliminary results.

I didn't like the idea of being in the hospital that long but I'd do it if it meant that I was guaranteed to beat this but there was no guarantee with clinical trials. The phase of this trial meant that they were attempting to show that the results were good enough to move to the next phase before submission to the FDA. It was quite possible that this could be a new treatment option for other AML patients and it could prove to be something that would offer new hope to someone like me.

Except, right now, it wasn't proven. The previous phase had only yielded the minimum positive results to move forward. It was a good thing that they'd chosen to move forward because it meant that the researchers and doctors in charge felt that this was a good chance for the treatment to have long term and far reaching effects. It could mean that I would be alive in a year but it could also mean that the trial wouldn't work and I'd be removed after the first three months. That would mean I'd have to find another trial or decide to not fight it and let the cancer do what it will.

I had spent hours now trying to make this choice and I still wasn't any closer to one than I was a week ago. There were just too many things to consider and I had no idea what the most important thing should be

I mean, obviously, what I wanted to do should come first and foremost but that was kinda hard when I didn't know what I wanted to do. Up until about ten minutes ago, I'd been pretty convinced that I didn't want to die. Now I wondered if it would be easier on everyone if I did. I wasn't sure my parents had the money to pay for a trial. We had great insurance but I was also sure that they were tired of keeping me alive and paying out the ass to do so. I also wasn't all that sure that I wanted to spend three months alone here in the hospital and then another seven after a two month reprieve.

My facetime rang, interrupting my thoughts. I sighed and answered it to find Wyatt lounging in his bed with my favorite up and coming independent artist, Winter Havens, playing loudly. I smiled immediately wishing that I could just lose myself in the music if only for a little while today.

"Hey girl, what's up?"

"Nothing," I lied.

"You sure about that?" He leaned closer to the camera and stared at me until I felt uncomfortable.

"No."

"Spill it."

I hesitated and then let it all fall out in one big jumble of word vomit. "The chemo didn't work. My cancer is still here and I have to decide if I want to do a clinical trial or if I want to die. There is no other option at this point. If I don't do the trial I'm going to die. But…I may not get into a trial. Just because I choose one, doesn't mean they are going to accept me and Dr. Morales can only fight for me so much before she has to stop and we have to move on. Mom said it's my choice but I know damn well that she wants me to choose a trial. I've spent hours now trying to figure this out and I'm still not any closer to a decision."

"Hold on….Just a minute, November. Slow down."

I was crying uncontrollably by then and shook my head while wiping my eyes. Nothing he was going to say was going to make a difference but I shut up and listened.

"There are more choices than just one. You just need to take a moment and breathe and let yourself grieve the fact that your cancer is still here. It's okay to be upset."

"I'm not upset. I'm pissed. What the fuck am I supposed to do, Wyatt?"

"What do you want to do?"

"If I knew that things would be a lot easier, wouldn't they?"

"Listen," he spoke softly. "Let me ask you something that may help."

"What?"

"November, do you really want to give up and die? Are you ready to tell Cancer that she won?"

I took a deep breath and slowly blew it out. I hung my head and shook it. Then I looked back up at him and whispered, "No."

"Then the decision is easier than you think. You know what you have to do. The hard part is over."

"The hard part is over?" I repeated with sarcasm. "Are you kidding me? How does not wanting to die make the decision easier? Am I just supposed to figure it all out now? It's somehow easier because I don't want to die? I've never wanted to die, Wyatt. Not since I was eleven years old and sitting on that doctor's table hearing the word cancer and not even knowing what it meant. But guess what. I AM DYING. You are too. Nearly every damn kid on this floor is dying and no one seems to really care other than us."

"That's not really fair, November. And just so we are clear, I'm not dying. I'm fighting and you're going through a lot right now and I'm trying to help."

"Well, you're not so stop."

"Now you're just being selfish and honestly, I don't think I want to see you anymore tonight."

He hung up on me and I screamed again. It seemed to be the only thing that helped today so I just kept on screaming.

Once I was done throwing my tantrum, I knew he was right. He'd forced me to face the fact that I didn't want to die. That should make my decision easier but it didn't. I could still die even with a clinical trial. Hell, the chances were just as high as not doing anything. The trial just gave me hope that I could fight this and win. Hope was important. Hope was what I needed right now and Wyatt had given it to me and I'd thrown it right back in his face like the selfish spoiled brat that I was. I hated myself for hurting him again. He'd only been trying to help me and I rewarded him with anger.

I prayed that he understood this wasn't the real me. I was going through a lot and I needed my friend and he was the only friend that I had. I didn't want to die. He was right. He was right about it all but now I couldn't even tell him that.

I needed to leave him alone the rest of the night, not because of what I'd done, but because he needed it and so did I. We both needed time to let things cool down before we spoke again so that we didn't ruin our friendship. It was what I was telling myself in order to keep myself from calling him or barging into his room.

I needed to sleep now. I needed to stop thinking, turn off my brain and rest so that tomorrow I could make the best decision possible. I couldn't delay it any longer. Every day was a day closer to death and I needed to wake up and face that consequence.

It was the last thought I had before my eyes closed and I fell into a restless sleep. My dreams were filled with clinical trials and funerals. I stood over my own grave and wept before finding myself in the hospital again starting a new trial. Each and every time I wound up at my grave and then it all reset and I started all over.

I stood in the back of my funeral and watched my parents cry. They were the only people that attended. Then I'd be seated next to them at my funeral as they celebrated the fact that their lives just got easier now that I was no longer a burden. My heart broke when I realized that they weren't sad at all that I was gone.

I ran from each funeral only to find myself standing at my grave. Sometimes it was covered in flowers and others it was bare and overgrown. It was as if no one visited it or cared that I was dead. Other times, the visitors were there in droves.

My subconscious was playing games with me and I wanted out of this dream world. I couldn't seem to wake up and felt trapped in this dream. I searched each scenario for Wyatt but he was never there. Maybe my mind was trying to tell me something but I wasn't going to give up on finding him. He had to be there somewhere. He wouldn't just give up on me and our friendship.

Looking for him helped to occupy my time in the dreams between funerals. For some reason I wasn't sad at any of them. I was torn between wanting my parents to miss me and for them to be thankful they didn't have to worry about me anymore.

I didn't want them to be sad when I was gone but I did want them to miss me some. My illness had been hard on them too and I just wanted them to find peace once I died.

My dreams were forcing me to deal with the things I couldn't when I was awake. My own mortality was something I wasn't sure I'd ever really be able to face in the daylight.

I woke, tired and irritable, but I had a choice to make and I was going to make it. Wyatt had been right, I didn't want to die yet and that was enough to figure out how to fight this war raging inside of me. Why the hell was he so smart?

I called my mother just after breakfast and asked her and Dad to come to the hospital. I asked Valerie if it would be possible to have Wyatt join me after I'd spoken to Mom and Dad alone. I wanted him to know my decision because he was a huge part of why I'd made it.

Mom and Dad arrived within the hour and both entered the room quietly. I could tell that they were worried about what I'd decided. I waited for them to get settled and held my breath for a few minutes before I spoke.

"I know you've been worried about me making this decision and I've listened to what both of you have had to say on the subject. I've also listened to Dr. Morales and looked over all of the information that she's given me. I studied every clinical trial available for AML and a few that weren't for AML." I laughed a little nervously then got right back to business.

"I've made my choice."

"And?" My father wasn't a patient man and my mother slapped his arm and shushed him.

"Go on, November."

"I chose a trial that if I get into starts within the month. The results have been good in the first few stages. It has the least side effects, or the least disgusting ones. It's also been the most requested trial so there is no guarantee that I'm going to get in and yes, I have chosen a second choice but it does have some nasty side effects and the results aren't as good."

My mother was on her feet hugging me before I could finish what I was saying. I hugged her back. She was relieved and frankly, so was I. This had been weighing on me for days and I was glad that it was over. Except, it wasn't over. Now came the part that would have us all on edge. Now, we waited to see if they'd choose me as a candidate for the trial. If not, I had other options but the longer we waited, the faster my cancer would spread. I didn't have the luxury of time to keep waiting.

"I've already let Dr. Morales know my top choice and alternative," I continued. "She has contacted the research team and drug manufacturers. We should know something within the week. Between now and then, I'll stay here and my blood work will be analyzed daily and I'll be given a complete physical. I'll see the cardiologist as well as a nutritionist as diet will play a huge part in the success of the trial. From here on out, everything changes. If I'm selected, I'll start immediately. That means I'll be staying here for at least 3 more months. Dr. Morales doesn't think it would be a good idea for me to come home before the trial starts since there is widespread flu activity in the area. I'll go straight into isolation after today until the end of the trial to ensure that I'm at my healthiest."

"That's a lot to take in, November." My mother was quiet but firm. "Are you sure you're ready for all of this?"

"Don't start doubting now, Mom. I've been in isolation before. I know what to expect and I can facetime every day. This is the best choice for me. I don't want to die and this is my only option to make sure that doesn't happen.

The knock on the door startled my parents but I called out for the nurses to let Wyatt in. He stopped just inside the door and said hello to my parents and exchanged small talk for a few moments before looking at me questioningly.

"Come on in and sit down. I have some news."

I waited for him to find a spot and settle down before I looked at my mother and waited for her to take a seat as well.

"Mom and Dad know already, but I wanted to tell you since you were a big help in getting me to this decision. I've decided to try a clinical trial. I'm going to fight to live thanks to you reminding me what I was fighting for. So, thank you, Wyatt. Without you, I wouldn't be ready to face this battle."

The smile that lit up his face said it all. He was happy that I'd made the right choice.

"It's about damn time, November."

"Oh, shut up."

"So, are you going to get to go home before it all starts?"

I shook my head. "Nope, I'm stuck in here and you're stuck with me."

He rolled his eyes and we both laughed. "Could be worse, I guess."

Now that the decision was made, we could all breathe a sigh of relief but it was far from a done deal. Dr. Morales would go before the committee on Monday and state my case. She would be armed with all of my blood work results over the last year, my original diagnosis and all of the results from following relapses. I wasn't a prime candidate for this trial simply because my rate of relapse was high, but she felt that given the right information the team would see that I was a good fit.

I was young, and they didn't have anyone my age on the trial. They also had no one with as many relapses as I had and that was something that could really help should I respond well to the trial. The more information we were armed with the better. Now we waited until the committee was done with their decision.

I didn't want to stress and worry so I made everyone involved swear that we wouldn't mention the trial more than twice a day and we would focus more on having fun and making the most of the time I was stuck in isolation.

We settled on a Facetime schedule so that my parents could stay informed and I could have time to talk to Wyatt. The nurses even agreed that it would be fine for Wyatt to visit and stay just outside the doorway.

Mom decided to run out and stock up on snacks and extra coloring books and actual books to keep me entertained in down times. She even surprised me with some new movies and a few gift cards to iTunes so I could get some new apps and games.

Wyatt and Dad jumped to their feet to help her with the large cart of things she wheeled in. I exclaimed in shock that she had so much stuff.

"Mom, did you buy out the entire WalMart?"

"I only got things you're going to need, November. Now, help me figure out where to put the snacks."

The small closet in the room wasn't anywhere near large enough for what she'd bought and my clothes. Dad suggested that they run out and buy storage bins and I simply shook my head in amusement. It was just like my parents to insist that I have everything I could ever need or want while stuck here in the hospital. I didn't argue with them because they wouldn't listen anyway.

Dad gave my mom a quick kiss and off he went to pick up storage bins for my room. I guess this was what it would have been like if I had been going off to college instead of this so I let him go. I didn't want to miss the experience that I wouldn't ever get and for now I could just pretend this was my college dorm.

Essentially my parents were leaving me here to learn, perhaps not the traditional subjects but I believed wholeheartedly that I would learn more with this clinical trial than I ever would have in school. I wouldn't have as much fun but who needed fun when it meant you were going to be alive at the end?

While Mom, Wyatt and I continued to put away all the stuff that mom insisted I needed, we talked about how good this was going to be for me. Wyatt seemed extra quiet but I wouldn't have a chance to ask him about what was going on until well after Mom and Dad left.

Hours after I'd announced my decision, I was finally alone in my room and sank down into a chair, tired and hungry. Dad had picked up my favorite burger and fries with a milkshake for me just before they left and I was ready to devour it. I'd just unwrapped my burger when one of the night nurses, Nicole, appeared in the room to take my vitals.

"Hey, kiddo, that looks delicious. Mind if I get some vitals before you dig in?"

I obliged because what choice did I have? She took my blood pressure, temp and pulse then jotted it all down on her little scrap of paper. "Everything looks great. You need anything?"

"Nope, I think I'm good for now."

"You look tired, try to get to bed early. See you in a few hours."

She waved as she closed the door behind her and I thought about how nice all of the nurses on this unit were. I wouldn't have made it without them and their kindness. They'd been there on my hardest days and never let me forget what I was fighting for. They'd sat with me when I was sick and laughed with me when I was well. They truly were some of my best friends and I was grateful I had them in my life.

I finished my dinner and did exactly as Nicole suggested. I climbed into my bed and lay back to watch some tv before bed. I wasn't really invested in the sitcom on the tv but it filled the silence of the room. I was almost asleep when Wyatt Facetimed.

"Hey," I said sleepily, rubbing my eyes.

"Hey, were you already asleep?"

"Almost, but it's okay. What's up?"

"Nothing really. Just got off the phone with my 'rents."

"Oh? Where are they this week?" I tried not to sound harsh but his parents really annoyed me by not being here.

"The Bahamas. Dad has some clients there or something."

"Must be nice. Are they coming to see you soon?"

He quietly shook his head. "Probably not. Mom said they are heading to Germany after this. They want to check on the house there and spend some time with friends."

"Of course, that makes all the sense in the world."

“Don’t November.”

“I’m sorry,” I said, not really meaning it. “I just hate that they aren’t here for you.”

“Yeah, me too, November, but I can’t change it so it is what it is.” Wyatt’s voice cracked with disappointment and it broke my heart.

“I’ll share my folks with you. They’ll be happy to have someone to dote on while I’m in isolation. You’ll get some good food and games out of it.”

“Sure, that sounds great.” His voice betrayed him but I let it slide without mentioning it. I didn’t want him to know that I heard the hurt in his voice or saw the tears in his eyes. He was still a guy after all.

“I’ll let them know tomorrow. They’ll be thrilled. I bet Dad will be here for the football game tomorrow night. He’s a diehard Eagles fan.”

“Eagles? Really? Oh man, we’re gonna have to talk.” He laughed and I was happy to hear it.

“Wyatt,” I said hesitantly.

“Yeah?”

“Thanks for being here.”

“Same to you. Maybe when we’re out of here, I can take you to a movie or something.”

“Why Wyatt, are you asking me on a date?” I feigned shock and clutched at my non-existent pearls.

“Are you saying yes?”

“Yeah, I think I am.”

“Good. I’d hate to have to beat up any other guy who thinks he can take my girl out.”

My smile widened and I went to bed that night warm in the thoughts of being Wyatt’s girlfriend. I’d never had a boyfriend before but everything in me screamed with happiness. He was everything I could have wished for.

Chapter Nine

I woke up the next morning still smiling. I immediately texted my parents and let them know that Wyatt had requested that they step in for his parents. My Dad texted back right away saying he'd be down for the game that evening just as I had suspected. Mom was excited to have someone to sit with at the hospital so she could keep an eye on me while hanging with Wyatt.

I texted Wyatt and dug into my breakfast as soon as it was delivered. I was starving and it was waffles, my favorite. My mouth was full and I had syrup all over my face when I answered Wyatt's Facetime.

His laughter filled the room as soon as he saw me.

"As soon as I ask you to be my girl, you let yourself go. Where did the mystery go, November?"

"Oh, shut up," I laughed, my mouth still full and chewing.

"There's the girl I love."

As soon as he realized what he'd said, he blushed and so did I. I swallowed the waffle and stared at him silently for a few seconds.

"You……love me?"

"Yeah, I do."

"Wow."

He stared at me and shook his head.

"I love you too," I hurriedly replied, realizing I hadn't said it back. "Sorry, you sorta caught me off guard."

"I caught myself off guard," he explained. "I wasn't planning on telling you that right away, but what the Hell, it's true."

"You're my first boyfriend."

"Ever?"

"Ever."

"Shit." He let it digest and frowned. "That's hard to live up to."

"I don't have anyone to compare you to, so you'll be fine."

"I've had other girlfriends, November. Are you okay with that?"

"Are you still seeing them?"

"No."

"Then, I'm fine with it."

"I'm not a virgin, either."

"Well, keep it in your pants. I'm in isolation." I laughed and smiled at him. "Seriously, I already kinda knew that. You're kinda hot, you know."

"I wish I was. I wish you were my first."

"Stop it, Wyatt. We're not talking about sex right now. We're both taking chemo, well, you know what I mean. We can't have sex right now."

"November," he lowered his voice to a whisper. "I'd fuck you right now if I could."

I feigned shock at his language and we both burst into laughter.

"Okay, change of subject needed," I said.

"Fine. What movies are you watching today?"

"Well, first day in isolation tradition says it has to be "Weekend At Bernies"."

"What the Hell is that?"

"Oh my Gods, Wyatt, how have you never seen the best movie ever made?"

"Because I'm not 140 years old?"

"Neither am I but I've seen it at least 100 times now. My Dad loves it and so do I."

"Well, what's it about?"

"So this guy Bernie dies, right? And his two employees show up at his house for the weekend and find him dead. Well, they don't want to be accused of killing him, so they decided to pretend he's still alive and hilarity ensues. You HAVE to watch it."

"Maybe. But today is all about Tom Cruise movies for me. I'm going to start with Risky Business and Top Gun."

"Do you have snacks? If not, I might know where you can get some."

We both fall into fits of laughter again and I can't help but feel happier than I've ever been. Was this what being in love was like? Was what Wyatt and I had actually love? Or were we simply latching onto one another because we were both dying? It was easy to do when you were stuck in the hospital. I'd seen many failed "relationships" over the years I'd spent here. Even the doctors and nurses weren't immune to it.

I shook that thought from my mind because I didn't want to ruin my good mood. Wyatt was my boyfriend and that was all that mattered.

Nurse Valerie popped up on Wyatt's screen and I waved. "Hey November, I'll be in to see you shortly. Right now though, we need to cut this off so I can get Wyatt's vitals."

"If we must," I said in response. "See ya, Wyatt."

"See you, November," he said with a wink and the screen went black.

I decided to get up and shower while I waited for Valerie to make her rounds. The heat from the water was soothing and I hummed while I showered. I'd just finished dressing and was brushing my hair out when Valerie finally made her way into my room.

"Looks like you made good use of your time." She quickly began to jot down notes off the IV pole I was attached to. "Can I get your blood pressure and temp?"

"Sure thing,"

Once she'd finished taking notes on my vitals she sat down on the edge of the bed and took the brush from my hand and began to brush the tangles from my hair.

"Thanks," I said with a smile.

"So, tell me about what's going on with you and Wyatt."

"There isn't much to tell. He's nice and I like him."

"And go on."

"And today he asked me to be his girlfriend." My excitement couldn't be contained and Valerie smiled brightly.

"Just be careful, November. Relationships that start in hospitals usually end in heartbreak."

"Valerie, we're both dying of cancer. Neither of us have any expectations, I assure you."

"You're a smart girl. I have no doubt you've thought this through but I also know that at your age, love is new and it's powerful and beautiful and you just want to feel all warm and fuzzy and spend all of your time with him. I know all about it. I just don't want either of you to get hurt."

"It's not like we can actually even see one another except through Facetime. I'm stuck in isolation and he has four more rounds of chemo."

She gave up the argument and stood up. "Okay, I give. I've got to go record all of these vitals in charts before I get in trouble. They'll be in to get some blood soon. Until then, try to get some rest. Maybe spend some time out of the bed and read over by the window or something. Buzz if you need anything."

WIth that she was out of the room before I could reply. I took her advice and grabbed my copy of the latest James Patterson novel and curled up in the chair. The warmth of the sun had me nodding off within the hour and I let my head fall back on the chair and enjoyed the nap.

I only woke up when lunch was delivered. Once the tray was dropped off I realized how hungry I was. The chicken sandwich and salad looked amazing and I quickly ate it all. I was still hungry and I was digging through the snacks my mom had left when I stopped to laugh at how she'd just known that I'd want them. She was brilliant, my mother.

I hadn't spoken to Wyatt since early this morning but I wasn't worried. We'd both planned to spend the day watching movies so I figured that's what he'd been doing. On top of that, my father was due to spend some time with him today.

After I found a snack, I went back to my chair and my book. It wasn't long before I fell asleep again. Being stuck alone in a hospital room was exhausting and I was currently catching up on my sleep.

Dinner arrived and woke me up again. I'd slept the day away but the sunlight had been so warm and the chair comfortable. I checked my phone and saw six texts from Wyatt, one from my dad and three from my mom. I read through them while I ate the turkey and mashed potatoes I'd ordered for tonight's dinner. It reminded me of Thanksgiving and I realized that I was going to miss the big dinner again this year. I'd probably miss Christmas too.

Wyatt's texts were full of movie talk and telling me how my dad had really shown up and that they were playing Connect Four and my dad was winning. He told me he loved me at the end of each text and I smiled to myself as I typed back a quick 'I love you too' and 'Have fun.'

Dad's text was just a quick hello and that he'd stop to wave from the door before he headed home. I was sure that he'd already opened the door and found me sleeping and left me to it.

Mom's were full of questions and reminders to eat and stay hydrated. I was certain she would call before bedtime and remind me of those things once more. It was killing her that she couldn't be here and I needed to be nice to her when she did call. She was worried and I had to remind myself of that often or I'd forget what it was like for her.

Sometimes I thought I had the easy part. I stayed in the hospital and got the treatments but Mom sat beside me and worried about her firstborn child. She worried every second of every day; even the days that were good and I was in remission, she still worried.

I only had to worry about cancer but Mom had to worry about my cancer, my sister, my dad, our home, me, and everything else that moms had to worry about. She sat with me all day and somehow still managed to keep our house clean, get groceries, cook dinner, show up for Tracy at school events, and make sure my father was happy. She took care of us all and she did it without any complaint.

I wondered how many nights she'd cried in Dad's arms after I was diagnosed. Did she scream and wail? Did she question God's plan the way that I did? Would she be okay when I died? Would any of them be okay?

I had to stop thinking about those things. I wasn't planning to die anytime soon, though I guess when you were terminal you were always thinking about death. But thinking about death didn't help much when you were fighting to avoid it at all costs.

I finished my dinner, pushed thoughts of death from my mind and turned on the TV to find something to take my mind off of things. I found some old sitcom and settled in, laughing at the funny situations the people were put into.

I almost thought I could hear my dad and Wyatt yelling at the football game down the hall. Around 9pm my dad poked his head into the doorway and waved.

"Hey, baby girl! How ya feeling? Missing us yet?"

"Hey, Daddy. Of course I'm missing you. I slept most of the day because there was no one to play board games with or talk about nothing with. I'm feeling okay. Just bored and already ready to come home."

"You have a long way to go, honey. Try not to think about it. Did you talk to your mom today?"

"I did. She wanted to know everything I ate and what my book I'm reading is about. You know how Mom is."

"I sure do, but she means well. Go easy on her. It's hard on her when she's not able to be here with you. Just give her a break sometimes and maybe tell her that you love her. Okay, honey, I gotta run before the nurses kick me out. I love you and I'll text you in the morning. Try to get some sleep and maybe let Wyatt get some too. He seemed a little worn down today.I love you."

"Night, Daddy. I love you more."

I was suddenly bummed that he was gone. I truly missed my dad staying the night with me and my heart hurt. I knew it wouldn't be forever but it didn't lessen the pain of him leaving that evening. My heart missed him and a tiny part of me worried it would be the last time I'd get to see him. My dad was amazing. I was the luckiest girl alive to have him for a father.

I took his advice and let Wyatt rest. I was convinced that he'd been putting on an act of being okay after his first round of chemo. Round two started in two weeks. His therapy was intense due to the nature of his tumor and his type of cancer.

I was really worried about him. I wish I knew the true nature of his cancer but it wasn't my place to question his medical procedures or his doctors; even though I wanted to. I didn't know his doctor or the type of therapy he was taking other than his chemo. I was sure he was on daily medication as well and that medication was key to his recovery. Maybe he'd trust me enough someday to tell me about his health care and his plans in case this therapy didn't work.

I hated that I thought about his medical care before I thought of his family or friends. But this was who we were. We were cancer patients before we were human it seemed most days. Our lives revolved around cancer and fighting cancer. There was never a single moment where our cancer wasn't forefront in our lives. Everyone I knew always asked about my cancer when they spoke to me or my family. We were the face of cancer for everyone who knew us right now.

And it sucked.

There wasn't anything we could do about it simply because everyone wanted to know how the cancer kids were doing. We had to grin and bear it when random people dropped by to gawk or check on us, even when we didn't know who they were. It was a fact of cancer, like it or not.

Many times we were the kids they paraded out or talked about when they wanted people to feel sorry for them or for us. We were used to getting people to donate money to some charity or for those who knew us to feel good about themselves that they did something nice for the dying kids.

Most of the time we weren't seen or heard, we were simply a part of the family that wasn't discussed unless they had to. We felt left out and unwanted by everyone except our parents if we were lucky enough to have parents who stayed with us. Wyatt wasn't one of those kids so I couldn't imagine how it felt for him.

We didn't go to traditional school, but instead we were homeschooled or had a homebound teacher who came to the hospital and gave us special privileges like open book exams. We usually needed that open book too because our memories weren't the best. The drugs they gave us helped us forget how sick we were, but they also made us forget a lot about our day to day lives as well.

We were constantly being told by our peers that we were lucky we didn't have to go to school every day. Us cancer kids would have given anything in the world to be healthy enough to complain about having to ride the bus and be in a classroom all day. I know I had cried many nights because I wanted to be normal and go to school and make friends. Even when I was healthy I wasn't allowed in the public school setting. There were too many germs and viruses that I could catch that would be so much worse for me thanks to the chemo destroying my immune system.

So many people had no idea how lucky they were to have normal boring and tedious lives. I would have given anything for a normal life. I may have been the only kid in the world who actually wanted to go to school instead of staying home. I'd had more than my fair share of days laying on the couch eating chicken soup and watching game shows.

Not that I didn't have school. Mom had arranged for a nice lady to come in three times a week to teach me. She worked for the schools and I was on a program called "homebound". Basically it meant that I got special treatment when it came to taking exams or if I was taking chemo or in the hospital I didn't even have to take them.

Some days I wondered if they just passed me because they felt sorry for me. Mom told me that wasn't the case and that I had to learn the material and prove that I knew it before they'd pass me. I'd tested that theory out once in the ninth grade. I chose 'C' for all of the answers on my test. I didn't even read the questions. I passed with a B.

Of course, I didn't tell my mom about that. She'd have insisted that I retake it and be graded properly on the work. I wasn't that stupid. I had proven my point to myself and that was what mattered.

I'd been on homebound since I was eleven. At this point I knew I wasn't going to college and that I probably wouldn't live long enough to graduate even if I could go. I didn't have a goal for my future because I'd been told for so long that I didn't have a future.

Or I didn't have one until I'd met Wyatt. Now I wanted to live long enough to go on that date with him. It's all I had thought about since he'd asked me.

My mind raced and I started putting a plan together. One way or another, I was going to have that night with Wyatt. I'd make sure of that.

Chapter Ten

A few days had passed since my dad had been to visit Wyatt and things were good. Wyatt and I talked every day, all day and he seemed to be in good spirits even though he had another round of chemo coming up quickly. Some of his friends had been by to visit him and that seemed to help him stay positive and have a good outlook on how this next round would go. He hadn't mentioned his parents since their phone call and I didn't dare to bring them up.

We spent our time watching movies over Facetime and laughing at the silliness of old sitcoms we found on the hospital tv. He was my best friend and I was so glad that he was here to help pass these days in isolation.

We were in the middle of watching Weekend At Bernies again when Dr. Morales, Valerie and Cynthia came through the door.

I told Wyatt that I would call him back and turned to face Dr. Morales and crew. They had serious looks on their faces and that scared the daylights out of me.

"November, we have some news," Dr. Morales said without betraying any emotion.

"About the trial?"

"Yes."

"Just tell me. If it's bad I can handle it."

Dr. Morales pulled a chair up close to my bed and sat down. She opened the folder in her hands and studied it for a minute before she spoke again.

"The team and I met yesterday and went over your medical history and your treatment history. They didn't like some of the numbers they were seeing from recent blood work but they felt that we could get those numbers where we need them to be in time. I got the call about ten minutes ago. You've been accepted into the clinical trial."

I sat in stunned silence and stared at her in disbelief. This was the news I had so desperately wanted to hear but for the time being it didn't register in my brain that I heard her correctly.

"We have to start preparing you immediately for the next steps," she continued on. "We're going to start you on iron and increase your potassium levels. This trial drug is harsh and there are going to be some side effects that aren't going to be fun. Are you up for this?"

I nodded. "When do I start?"

"We have three weeks to get you ready. The team wants to come in and meet with you before the trial begins so that you are all on the same page. From here on out, your meals are going to be protein and veggie loaded. We need to get your weight up because this drug makes you lose weight and you can't stand to lose any. I need you to gain at least 10-20 pounds but I need you to do it in a healthy way. Snacks, meals, shakes are all on the menu. Today is the last day you can just order what you want from the cafeteria so I suggest you order all of your favorites. From here on out you're on a meal plan. The team also wants you to do another round of chemo prior to the start of the trial."

I looked at her questioningly, waiting for her to understand what she'd just said.

"I know, chemo typically makes you lose weight. But we are going to make sure that doesn't happen this time, as best as we can anyway."

"So you're a real life witch now? You can control how chemo makes me puke? Shit, why weren't you doing that all along Doc?"

"Very funny." She didn't laugh, instead continuing on. "We will be giving you anti nausea meds with the chemo in large doses. I need you to eat no matter how you're feeling. If you want this trial to work, you have no other choice, November."

She paused and waited for me to respond. I did not say a word. I've done this chemo thing many, many times since I was eleven years old and I knew damn well that gaining weight on chemo without the use of steroids was going to be hard.

"I can almost read your mind," she stated matter-of-factly. "No, we are not going to be giving you prednisone to help. We cannot compromise your health in any way and I surely don't want steroids to be the reason you can't do this trial. You simply have to try your best to eat at least two meals a day on chemo."

"When does this all start?"

"Chemo starts tomorrow, so get some rest tonight. It's going to be an aggressive round and we're going to get your platelets in before we start. The order is in and they should be here by tomorrow morning. Once they are done, you will have a few hours to rest and eat, then before bed tomorrow night, we start this round of chemo. I want you to be prepared, November. This is going to be extremely aggressive. You're going to hate your life and me before the five days are done and that's okay. Once done, we have two weeks to get you built back up enough to start the trial. Are you up for this?"

"Yes." I spoke calmly and with certainty. I was prepared for anything as long as it meant I didn't die before I got to go on that date with Wyatt.

"That's what I wanted to hear. I took the liberty of ordering you a giant ice cream sundae for after dinner tonight. One last treat before we get serious."

"Thank you, Dr. Morales."

"Any questions?"

"Have you told my parents any of this yet?"

"No, I wanted you to hear it all and make your decision to do this before I called them."

"They aren't going to be happy that you're trying to kill me before you save me, Doc."

"They will have to get the Hell over it, won't they?"

Everyone in the room laughed and it lightened the mood.

"Alright, kiddo, I have to get some vitals and Cynthia is going to get some blood, okay?" Valerie was already putting the blood pressure cuff on me as she spoke.

Doctor Morales waited while Cynthia and Valerie did what needed to be done and then waited for them to leave so she could speak to me privately.

"Listen November, this is going to be the hardest few weeks of all of your chemo rounds. I can't promise you it's going to be easy to be in this trial but I definitely think it's going to be worth it. I fought hard to get you in and the team is excited to see the research on someone your age and how you handle it. This could be huge for everyone involved. Please be easy on yourself and when you're having a bad day, speak up. I've put a team on standby for you that includes therapists you can talk to and psychiatrists that can prescribe medication for anxiety or other issues that may arise. Just don't get lost in how you're feeling because that's just part of this entire thing. You have to let me know when things are bad so we can fix them for you."

"Okay," I said quietly.

"The team wants to meet with you after this last round of chemo to see how you're doing and to officially meet you. They know a lot about you medically and about your life as well but they don't know you the way we do, November. Let them see why we fought so hard for you and I promise you they will do everything in their power to make this trial a success for you and them. Your success is their success."

"I understand."

"Okay. You have my cell number if you need anything. Don't hesitate to call or ask a nurse for something. I have a script in for a sleeping aid for you tonight. I need you well rested for tomorrow."

She was just about to close the door when she turned around and smiled. "By the way, Wyatt is looking good and it appears he is handling his treatments like a champ."

My smile brightened and she closed the door quietly behind her. She'd left me with a lot to think about and I was overwhelmed but thankful that I didn't have to be the one to relay all of the information to my parents. Telling Wyatt was going to be difficult enough because he was going to ask questions that I may not have answers to. There was no easy way to tell him but at the same time, he would want to know. How soon I'd tell him was the question. If he asked my dad, and he spilled the beans before I told him, Wyatt would be hurt and I didn't want that. I also didn't want my parents asking a lot of questions about me and Wyatt. I wasn't ready to tell them everything just yet.

As far as they knew, we were just friends and I wanted to leave it that way for now. My mother would make a huge deal over him being my boyfriend and tell me that right now I needed to be focused on this trial and my health and that boys would come later when this was all over.

The only problem with that logic is that when this was all over, I may be dead. And I like him.

A lot.

So not telling them was the best bet. If Dad knew, he'd tell Mom. So that was not an option at all. If I told Tracy, she'd tell them both. Besides Tracy and I weren't close like that. I'd never confided in her, nor her in me. Some days I forgot I had a sister. I didn't see her that much and she lived a life I knew nothing about. It's just how it was when you were the cancer kid.

So I'd just keep Wyatt and my relationship to myself. That meant that I could enjoy it without anyone else's opinions on it and I could be happy. And right now, happy was important.

I fell asleep thinking about him that night. By morning I was ready to conquer cancer once and for all but I still wasn't ready to tell Wyatt about the trial's rules and such. That would just have to wait another day.

Breakfast came right on time and my stomach growled at the smell of it. The tray was loaded with turkey bacon and an egg white omelet with a side of fresh fruit and orange juice. Whole wheat toast with butter and jelly were on the tray as well and I devoured it all.

Valerie popped in right as I was finishing up with a big smile behind her mask.

"Hey, kiddo, how's my favorite patient this morning?"

"Good and stuffed."

"Well that's good. We're gonna get some vitals, some blood and you're on the schedule for platelets at eleven."

"Sounds like a plan. What time is chemo scheduled to start?"

She shuffled some papers before answering. "Looks like six tonight provided the platelets are on time and you're feeling good."

"Do I get to eat before they start?"

"Yes, ma'am. Nutrition will be sending up some protein shakes in a little while as well. I'll label them and put them in the break room fridge for you. Dr. Morales has you on a schedule for them three times a day from here on out."

"She's trying to fatten me up like the Thanksgiving turkey."

I laughed but I was worried and Valerie was too.

"We'll get you where you need to be. Have you filled Mr. Hotness down the hall in?"

"No, not yet. I don't wanna answer his questions right now."

"Well, he asks about you anytime one of us comes into the room so you may want to fill him in before someone slips up and tells him for you."

"Shit."

"Language," she said laughing and jotting down things on her scrap of paper.

"Yeah, yeah. I'm dying. I can cuss all I want."

"You're not dying today, so watch your language."

"Yes ma'am."

Valerie winked and waved before heading out to finish her rounds and I tried to summon up the courage to call Wyatt. Time passed me by while I was trying to find that courage and before I knew it lunch had arrived and so had my platelets. They were late, as usual, but at least they made it today.

I had just opened my salad when Wyatt called.

"Hey, you avoiding me?"

"Like you could get rid of me even if you wanted to." I joked. "It's just been kind of busy in here."

"Oh?"

He waited quietly for me to go on and I just let the words fall out of my mouth. I told him everything that Dr. Morales had told me the day before and how scared I was that this wasn't going to work and that I was going to die anyway.

"Stop, November. You can't think like that. If you keep saying that, you're going to die and then I'm going to be pissed. You can't leave me. Promise me."

"Wyatt, you know I can't make that promise. I may not be able to keep it."

"But I also know that you'll do everything within your power to keep it."

"Damn it Wyatt, I can't promise that. I don't want to hurt you."

"The only way you're going to hurt me is to leave me."

"I'm not going anywhere, if I can help it. I'm here now, let's just enjoy it."

"When do you start the chemo?"

"Tonight. When is your next round?"

"Starts tomorrow. I guess we can be miserable together, babe."

"You know what they say, the couple that pukes after chemo together, stays together."

"Until death parts them."

"Now who's talking about death?"

We both laughed but it wasn't the kind of laughter that was because you found something funny. It was the kind where you laughed because if you didn't, you may cry.

We did our best to change the conversation after that, but it was hard to focus on anything else that day. After lunch I had to say goodbye so I could be hooked up to the platelets and I was only about ten minutes into the transfusion when Dr. Morales stopped in to check on me.

"How are you feeling, November?" She was already checking my chart so I knew that she knew everything already but she waited impatiently for me to answer.

"Fine."

"Good. Nothing unusual has come up, right?"

"Nope. I've eaten and I feel perfectly fine. Why?"

"Just making sure. Once the transfusion is done, I want you to sleep some. I need you well rested to start this chemo tonight."

"You've made that clear already, Doc."

"November, you're more than just a patient to me. I worry about you more than I should but you remind me of my daughter and I don't want anything to happen that can ruin this chance for you."

"I swear, I'm fine. I'd tell you if I wasn't. I know how important this is for the trial."

"That's good to hear. I want you to take this seriously."

"Do you really think this is going to work?" I needed to know.

She hesitated before she answered. "I'm not God or psychic but I truly believe this trial is your best chance at beating cancer and living a normal life."

"Normal isn't the goal, Doc. I want to live an extraordinary life. One where I'm happy and chasing dreams and never worrying about dying before I get married or have sex."

She chuckled and nodded, a smile forming on her face. "Well, let's see if we can make some of those dreams a reality. I'm going to send Val in with a protein shake for you then I want you to nap. Not just lay there and talk to that boyfriend of yours but actually sleep. You're going to need all of your strength in the coming weeks."

"Aye, Aye Captain." I saluted and we both laughed. But we both knew that she was right. I was in for the fight of my life and it started today. There was no time to worry or second guess anything. Now was the time to prepare for the coming war. And it was a war I intended to win.

Chapter Eleven

Day four of chemo was here and it was just like days one through three. I puked and cried and moaned and wished for death more times than I could count. Even though I knew that what was happening was needed to prepare my body for the clinical trial I was about to start, I couldn't help but wonder if maybe Dr. Morales was trying to kill me instead of keeping me alive.

This was pure madness and I was slowly drifting away into it. I was barely holding onto the life raft and had it not been for the nurses, my parents and Wyatt, I was sure I would have given up. As it was, my grip on reality was less than steady and I was starting to hallucinate or something.

I could have sworn that Wyatt was standing at the foot of my bed at some point during the night. I could almost feel his hand on my leg as he spoke softly and encouraged me to fight through this. His words comforted me enough that I could sleep a little then. I held onto those words and his voice as if it were the only thing that could save me from drowning in a sea of misery.

Tomorrow would be worse and the days following would make me regret my decision to live but I would continue to fight for a life I wasn't promised. It was who I was.

The times I was awake were agony. Every muscle in my body was revolting and waging a war against the chemo. The chemo itself was relentless in its quest to destroy my good cells along with the cancer. It didn't care, as long as death lay in its wake.

The few moments I caught a glimpse of myself on trips to the bathroom scared me. I looked frail and like I was at Death's door. My naturally pale skin looked opaque and as if it would tear with a single touch. My eyes were sunken in and heavily lidded with dark circles under them. My hair was falling out at an alarming rate while my breath barely sustained me.

I couldn't remember the last time I'd eaten anything. I recalled Dr. Morales ordoring some kind of IV that would nourish my dying body. She was avoiding steroids for as long as humanly possible but I was beginning to think we were beyond that point.

I held onto thoughts of Wyatt and I dancing at Prom. It was nothing more than a fantasy that somehow my mind had confused with reality but nonetheless it forced me to keep fighting. It was something I wanted almost as much as I wanted to beat cancer. I wanted to know what it felt like to be in Wyatt's arms, to have him hold me and kiss me, to twirl around a dance floor with him in a long dress and know that he loved me more than anyone else.

These thoughts helped me through those hard days because Wyatt was what was keeping me alive at that moment. He didn't know it and maybe never would but he was there when I needed him the most. I would never let that go.
While I was fighting, Wyatt was living his own personal Hell with his chemo. He would tell me later that he had wanted to give up then. The pain and sickness were so bad for him in ways I would never understand because our treatments were so different as were our cancers. No one tells you these things when you get sick and make friends with other cancer kids.

Cancer isn't the same for anyone. It affects us all differently and we have to live with not knowing truly how it will affect us until we are in the midst of it. I think that's the hardest part. Each new chemo they give you can affect you differently.

Wyatt's regiment was stronger and had worse side effects than the types I'd taken previously. He had already lost his hair and had lost so much weight. He was nothing more than skin and bones now and it scared me.

Valerie had slipped up one night and mentioned that his cancer was terminal, his tumor inoperable now. They'd gotten as much of it out as they could during his last surgery. He'd told me himself that his tumor had wound its way through his brain and that there was no way they'd ever be able to remove it fully.

I guess at the time it didn't dawn on me that he would probably die from that tumor in his brain. Before long it would start to cause memory loss for him. He may even forget me. It was a chance we'd have to take because neither of us was willing to give up what we had just because cancer may take it away.

I hated the thought that he may die, even more than I hated that I may die. I don't know why I focused on that while I was in the midst of this horrifying experience with this round of chemo but it occupied my mind and kept me alive so I was thankful for the thoughts.

Just when I thought I would surely die from the poison they were filling my body with, I was done. I would spend the next week recovering. My body had been through Hell and it needed to rest. I spent two days asleep and woke up to a very worried Dr. Morales standing over my bed.

"Welcome back, you had me worried there for a minute."

I blinked and did my best to sit up in bed. "Why?" I asked, genuinely concerned.

"You've been out for two days and prior to that you haven't kept anything in your system for days on end. This round was harder on you than even I anticipated."

"How's Wyatt?" I didn't care about me, I cared about how he'd handled his treatment.

"Our young friend is just fine. A little worse for the wear and has a new appreciation for the nurses but he should bounce back just fine. He's been asking about you every day. It's nice to have some good news for him."

I breathed a sigh of relief and laid back down.

"I'm going to send Val in to got your vitals and get you up and into some clean pjs. Eat something for me, November, even if it's only a bite. You've lost too much weight this week."

As soon as Valerie had helped me change, I begged her to get my iPad and let me call Wyatt. Even as she shook her head she was handing it to me and sitting down to brush what little hair I had left.

He answered on the third ring and he looked marvelous. The smile lit up his face and mine and we talked over one another. Then we both laughed at how silly we were and I let him speak first.

"My God, you're beautiful."

"And you must be on some really good pain meds."

"November, it doesn't matter what you look like after chemo, you're still the most beautiful girl in the entire world to me."

"You say the most eloquent things, Wyatt."

Valerie stood at that precise moment and made a face. "Okay, y'all are sickening. I'm going to go out here with the adults who aren't in love. Behave. Both of you."

And with that, she was gone and I was alone with the boy I loved.

"Hey, there is something I want to do before this trial starts. Do you think you would be willing to help me out with it?"

"Sure, what did you have in mind and will it get us arrested?"

"Nah, we aren't going to jail or anything but it might get us in some trouble."

"Spill it," he said suddenly excited to hear the plan.

I laid it all out for him and he sat quietly listening until I was done.

"Are you sure, November?"

"Yeah. I may not survive this trial. I want to do this."

"And you knew I wouldn't say 'NO' so you asked me huh?"

"I mean, how could you say no to me?"

"I can't. That's the problem."

From there we worked out the details of the plan and before long it had all come together. We would have to wait several days before we could execute it due to both of us being sick but what was a few days, right?

Once it was settled, we went right back to our normal routine of watching movies and playing stupid games together onlline. I was never happier than when Wyatt and I were spending time together and we both seemed to forget how sick we were when we were together on Facetime.

We talked about how my Dad had been checking on it every evening after work. He told me that Dad peeked on me as well and never failed to stop a nurse to get the latest information regarding my treatments. Wyatt and my dad were becoming good friends and I was happy that was the case.

Wyatt needed a father figure in his life to teach him all the stuff men needed to know and my dad needed Wyatt to help him see past his own sick daughter. They were a match made in Heaven and it made my heart happy to know that they had one another.

He always seemed content when he talked about my dad. He said my dad had given him a book and that he'd been reading every night. Leave it to my dad to find a way to get Wyatt to read.

We talked about our favorite tv shows and he filled me in on what had been happening with The Kardashians. As much as he protested I think he was just as invested in their show as I was. He'd even gone so far as to follow them all on Instagram and TikTok.

All was right with the world, and with Wyatt around I found that I was happier and didn't feel as sick as when he wasn't. I ate more because he encouraged me to keep my strength up and I wanted to make him proud of me.

When he wasn't feeling well, I read to him to pass the time until he fell asleep. Then I would sit there and listen to him breathe because it meant he was still alive and that was what mattered most.

The days passed slowly but with each passing second we were closer to executing my plan. He asked me every day if I was sure it was what I wanted to do and reminded me that I was risking everything.

"It's worth it," I would tell him and he'd get a big goofy grin on his face and we'd go back to our game or whatever it was we were doing. I hated that I couldn't touch him. And I knew that he hated it just as much.

We wanted to truly be together but the Universe didn't seem to care what we wanted. There was also some nurse always around trying to make sure that the hormonal teenagers on the unit were behaving.

The days passed slowly as I continued my daily routine. My hair fell out until there was none left. This round of chemo had tried to take everything from me. Unfortunately for me, I am one tough fighter.

I spent the days reading and talking to Wyatt. The nurses continued to watch us closely as if they suspected we were up to something. Cynthia and Valerie always gave a knowing look when they entered my room.

I spoke with my parents daily, keeping them informed on how I was feeling and all the normal hospital gossip that my mother seemed to miss. She filled me in on what was going on in the neighborhood and with Tracy and her friends. For a brief second, I missed being a normal kid.

I was beginning to think that my plan would never work out or happen. Every passing day made it seem impossible. I would obsess about it every waking moment.

A few more nights passed and I was alone in my room when a note slipped under my door. I hurried to grab it before a nurse found it and smiled as I read the sloppy handwriting.

"Tonight. 8pm. Be ready. Open the door and wear what's in the bag. W."

It was all that I needed to know and I plotted how I was going to convince the nurse that I was going to bed early. I peeked at the online schedule and saw that it was Pam on duty tonight. She'd be hard to fool but I'd manage. I'd pretend that Wyatt and I had a fight or something. That was sure to keep her out of here. She hated weepy teenage girls.

In just a few short hours my plan would be realized and then what? I had no idea what to expect since Wyatt had insisted on handling all of the details for the night. I didn't argue with him because to be honest I'd had no clue on how I was going to make this happen.

But Wyatt, he just took charge and I let him go for it. He'd seemed to be happy to have the distraction and I wasn't about to take any happiness away from him. We'd barely had any time to talk this week because he was always busy planning something and I was busy with all the meetings and tests for the trial which started in four days.

I was starting to get nervous that it was never going to happen but also that it was happening so fast. In two days I met with the team and Dr. Morales and I had to be prepared.

Just after dinner I staged the scene for Pam's sake and she hurried through her rounds in my room and told me she'd see me a little after midnight and to go to bed because I was getting on her nerves.

It had worked. I was free till midnight. Now if only Wyatt was able to cause the distraction so I could escape this room in a few hours.

I hurried to shower. Once I was clean and smelling nice thanks to some lotion my mom had packed me, I slipped into the dress that had been in the bag he'd left hanging on the door to my room.

The pale blue of the dress made my eyes look bluer somehow but it was huge on me, by at least two sizes. It didn't matter at all though. Nothing was going to ruin this night. The dress made me feel beautiful and that was all that mattered. Tonight had to be perfect. I ran my hands over the silkiness of the dress, smiling at myself in the mirror as I put on some lipgloss and my hat to cover my bald head and slipped into my cutest slippers.

Just as I was finishing up I heard the commotion down the hall. I laughed and knew that was my cue to make a break for it. Peeking my head out the room, I saw that the coast was clear and I ran for the stairs. The door was closing behind me when Wyatt came running in and stopped dead in his tracks.

"Damnit November, you look beautiful."

He was standing before me in a tux that was one size too big and his own hat covering his bald head and I couldn't speak at all. He was the most handsome boy I'd ever seen and I was head over heels in love with him.

We stood for just a moment before we both realized where we were and he grabbed my hand and we hurried down one flight and out the door to the elevator. As soon as the doors opened we ran in and hit the door close button and Wyatt pushed the button for the roof level.

He continued to hold my hand and my breath wouldn't quite reach my lungs. I was so scared and so happy all at the same time. I had no idea what the night held beyond what I'd told him I wanted and I was ready for anything.

But.....

Nothing could have prepared me for what I saw when we stepped out onto the roof. Tiny fairy lights twinkled and lit up the roof like it was bathed in stars. Soft music floated in the air and there were pillows on the ground for us to sit on if we got tired.

Everything was beautiful and I was about to tell him so when he pulled me into his arms and kissed me for the first time. It was my first kiss and I didn't know what to do but Wyatt's lips and tongue taught me all that I needed to know. I clung to him and he to me. Our bodies melded together as if they were one and once he broke the kiss, we danced.

It was just like my dream.

Only better.

Being in his arms felt right and magical and I was happier than I'd ever been. We twirled around the roof to the sounds of the music. My dress floated around my ankles and Wyatt's hand in mine made everything so much brighter. We stopped to eat a little of the snacks that Wyatt's friends had helped deliver. They'd somehow managed to bring up fruit and sliders and salads. I hadn't met his friends yet but I hoped that they knew how appreciated they were for their hard work on this. We sat together and talked about nothing and everything. Wyatt and I were so alike and yet so vastly different. He was the darkness to my light, and I was the innocence where he was wise beyond his years. We talked of books and the stories inside of them that inspired us. We spoke of the future that we were looking forward to. He held my hand and kissed it softly from time to time.

He told corny jokes just to hear me laugh and I rested my head on his shoulder because I could and it felt right. The smell of jasmine filled the night air and I shivered a little against the breeze. It was then that he pulled me closer and wrapped a soft blanket around my shoulders. He bent his head to kiss me and I swear I felt Heaven in that kiss. Somehow he'd managed to see inside of my dream and make it a reality. I would never forget this night and how Wyatt made me feel. This rooftop was special and our love grew deeper here.

We looked out over the city and for once I didn't feel a need to be normal. I was happy to be the cancer kid who had found her soulmate in a hospital room just down the hall. He just happened to be a cancer kid himself and that made it all the more special for us. Our love grew from something dark and scary to be the bright light that we needed to carry on and fight.

I was more in love with Wyatt than I could have even dreamed and to be here, in his arms, knowing that he loved me in return was enough to make me ready to fight for my life and his. I wanted to be here to see him beat cancer. I wanted to be there when he was happy and when he was sad. I wanted to be his light in the darkness like he was for me. I wanted him to know that no matter what happens I'll be here every day, with the intent to make him happy.

We professed our love for one another again and then he kissed me again and I was lost in that kiss. But if being lost meant that I spent every second with Wyatt, then I never wanted to be found. He ran the back of his hand across my cheek gently, his eyes dark with love and desire.

I was a virgin but I'd asked him to make love to me tonight. That's how this had all come about. If I were going into this trial without knowing for sure that I'd survived, I wanted to be with him in all the ways that counted. I wanted him to feel how much he meant to me. Every girl remembers the first time she has sex, and mine was about to be perfect. Not because he'd worked so hard to make this a night to remember, but because it was with Wyatt and I knew that he loved me.

We sat together for a little longer, neither speaking of what was to come. We simply enjoyed being here. Before long Wyatt stood and offered me his hand. I took it and stepped into the best night of my life.

"November, I know that you wanted this to be a prom and that you wanted things to move further for us but I don't want the same thing that you do."

I blinked in disbelief, my heart sinking as he spoke. He didn't love me, not the way that I loved him and I was broken.

"Oh, no, no, not like that," he said hurriedly when he saw my tears. "Don't cry. I didn't mean it that way. God, November, don't you know how much I love you? You are everything I ever dreamed of. I am so in love with you. I don't want just tonight. I want your forever, November no matter how long that is. I just want to spend the rest of my life and yours with you."

He dropped to one knee and pulled out a small velvet box from his jacket and I couldn't believe what was happening.

"Marry me. Don't think. Just say yes. Say you love me and you want to be my wife and let's be married from this moment on. We don't know how much time we have left and I want to spend every second of that limited time knowing that you're my wife, November."

He waited and I couldn't speak for a few moments.

"YES!" I shouted it so loudly that the word echoed around us and he stood and picked me up and twirled me as he kissed me. He placed the ring on my finger and kissed me again. He'd given me so much more than I'd asked for and before the night was through, I'd be his in every sense of the word.
His smile lit up his face and he stood before me with such love shining in his eyes.

"I know it all seems crazy and we don't have a license or a minister or anything but I don't care. I want to marry you. Not because we could die tomorrow but because we could live. I want to live. With you. Let's just have the ceremony here and now. I'll say vows and you say some too and in our hearts and the eyes of whatever or whoever is in charge of this crazy world, you'll be my wife."

"Let's do it," I laughed, caught up in his excitement.

He took my hand in his and kissed my cheek before he spoke again.

"November, when I met you, my life changed for the better. I came into this hospital thinking I was losing something only to find myself face to face with my future. I vow to love you for the rest of our lives. I vow to make you laugh on the hard days, cry with you when you're down, hold your hand when chemo makes you puke and live with you because our days are precious gifts and I want you to remember how important your life is. I vow to kiss you every morning and just before bed every night. I love you so much, November. You are my forever."

I beamed at him, and cleared my throat trying to find the words to tell him how much I loved him.

"Wyatt, no matter if I live one more day or a thousand more, my love for you will never die. I never thought I'd find my soulmate in a hospital corridor but there you were, curly hair falling in your face, a smirk that said you wanted to be anywhere but here and I was a goner. Your laughter has brightened my world. Where I once only saw gray, I now see color because of you. You have given me more happiness in one night than I've had in my entire life. I vow to love you with strength and passion. I vow to remind you of these days when we're old and sitting on our front porch yelling at the grandkids. Loving you is the best thing that has ever happened to me. I love you more than words could express, Wyatt. You are my forever."

He kissed me then, and it was perfect. He was my husband and I, his wife.I didn't think about the consequences of our actions then. I didn't worry about my parents or my treatment or any of the cancer that ravaged our bodies. I lived in the moment with Wyatt and let him love me.

Wyatt and I made love that night, beneath the stars and I'd never been happier in my life. He was gentle and patient with me, allowing me to feel everything and telling me how much he loved me over and over. He called me his wife and he loved me in ways I didn't know were possible.

He'd given me a night to remember and in that moment I knew that no matter how long we lived, I'd love him for the rest of my life. He was my forever and I was happy.

Midnight came far too quickly and the fairy tale had to end. We raced back to our rooms before Pam found out that we'd been gone and he kissed me in the elevator. I would never have imagined that an elevator could be so romantic but I was a married woman now, and I guess it was. We stepped out of that elevator and stood for a very long time not wanting to let go of the magic we'd experienced up there on our rooftop. But the fairytale had ended for us, for now, and he pulled his hand away from mine, turning to leave.

"I love you," he said as we went our separate ways to our rooms. I watched him for longer than I should have and finally hurried off to my room.

I'd just barely made it to my bed when Pam came in and stared at me for a minute. She shook her head and took my vitals.

"You been running or something in here?"

"Nope, Wyatt and I watched a horror movie. Scared the daylights out of me."

"Well that explains why your heart is racing then. Get some sleep. Big day tomorrow."

Once she was gone I grabbed my journal and wrote down every single moment of the hours before. I wrote of a love so true and deep, wanting our children to know how this crazy life of ours had started. My journal was full of things about Wyatt but this night was different. I wrote of how we danced and ate. How he sang off key and I laughed at him. I wrote of the ways he looked at me, his love for me so clear in his gaze. I wrote of my love for him and how he'd saved me. Without him, I wouldn't have chosen to fight. I'd be on my deathbed now, no hope for a future. But he was here, and I was choosing to fight so that I could spend my days being loved by him. I laid my pen down and closed the journal, placing it on the tray next to my bed. I lay back onto my pillows and closed my eyes, thinking only of my husband, Wyatt before I fell asleep. The smile never left my face. I was at peace and in love and nothing else mattered.

Wyatt

The night before had been perfect. My friends had really come through. I'd married the woman of my dreams and made love to her until I memorized every curve of her body. Her smile had brightened my entire world and I was the luckiest man alive to get to be her husband.

I couldn't erase the smile from my face as I clicked on her name for the Facetime call. It rang several times before the notification came up that she was unavailable. I tried again and got the same message. I didn't worry because I knew that she had her meeting today and maybe she was still sleeping or they were already there.

Pam strolled in and gave me the side eye.

"You have that same stupid grin on your face that November had last night. What's up with you two?"

"Nothing," I lied. "Hey, is she already in her meeting?"

Pam looked over at me and shook her head. "Nope, they aren't scheduled til this afternoon."

"Have you been in to check on her this morning?"

"Not yet, you're first on my list then I'm headed over. Why?"

"She didn't answer my Facetime."

"Well that is strange but maybe she was in the bathroom and didn't hear it."

I frowned again. "Could you just go over and check on her now?"

"Wyatt, don't."

"Pam, please?"

I couldn't shake the feeling that something was wrong and I just needed her to go now to check on her. I needed to know that she was okay.

"Fine," she said and left the room.

A few minutes passed and then the call came over the speakers.

"Code Blue, Room 323."

November's room.

"Oh God. Please. Please."

My heart stopped and I dropped to my knees. This couldn't be happening. Not now. Not her. I begged a God I didn't believe in to save her, to let this all be a dream. How could he take her from me now? We were just starting our lives. She was going to finally beat this damned disease once and for all.

I scrambled to my feet and ran down the hall as fast as I could, stopping in the door frame of her room. She was on the bed with Pam giving her CPR and I was shoved aside as more nurses and doctors ran in. I heard their words but didn't understand anything they were saying. It all seemed so far away.

My heart stopped for seconds at a time and I begged them to save her, to bring her back to me. Finally someone noticed me in the door and slammed it in my face. I felt someone's arms around me, leading me to a chair. I looked up to find Valerie there with me.

“Come on, there is nothing you can do standing in that doorway, Wyatt. You gotta let them work.”

“She’s gone, Valerie. She’s dead.”

Valerie held me and let me cry. She didn’t say a word and I understood that she was heartbroken too. They’d all loved her but none like I had. I’d lost my best friend and my life all in one.

“I know. I know, honey, but they’re doing everything they can. She can still come back. We don’t know how long she’s been gone. We have to have hope.”

“I knew it this morning when she didn’t answer. Last night was so perfect. It was like she’d known all along that it would be her last. How can she leave me like this?”

To her credit she didn’t ask me until later what I’d meant. Hours passed and her parents came and her mother cried in the hallway while Mr. C held her.

The night before I’d held November like that, close, tenderly, our hearts filled with love. Within 12 hours I’d lost her and my heart was shattered. I’d only known her a few months but we’d lived an entire life inside these steril hospital walls. I’d fallen in love with her and married her. We’d made love and held one another until we fell asleep. She’d beamed with happiness when I had placed the ring on her finger. It had been my grandmother’s ring and I was sure my mother had thought I’d lost my mind when I asked for it but she’d made sure I’d gotten it.

She hadn’t asked many questions just for the name of the girl who would wear it. I’d given it to her and told her that I would marry her if it were the last thing I ever did. She hugged me. I couldn’t remember the last time my mother hugged me or even sat with me. But November had made that happen even if she didn’t know she had. She was magic, my wife.

I’d felt stupid, wondering if she’d say “yes”. I worried that she didn’t love me the way I loved her. I was nervous but I knew that if I didn’t ask her I’d regret it for the rest of my life. I don’t know how I could have doubted her. The love she’d shown me had been selfless and courageous considering the fight we both were in.

November is my best friend and the girl I love. Now I had to write a eulogy for her and it wasn't okay.

Mr. Collins came over to where I sat and sat beside me.

“Wyatt, are you okay?”

“No, not at all.”

“It’s okay son. It’s a hard day for us all, but I have a couple of questions.”

"Yeah, okay."

"The ring she wore?"

"Was my grandmother's. She said yes."

He pulled me into a hug and I let the tears fall. I'd been worried that he'd want to kill me for not asking him first but he comforted me. He'd lost his daughter, his baby girl and here he was offering me compassion and love.

"She loved you very much Wyatt. I saw it every time we mentioned your name. I'm so glad that in her last moments she knew love in return."

"I already miss her. Why?"

"I've been asking God that for a long time, son. I don't have answers for you. I just know that her short life meant everything to her mother and I. She fought long and hard and we were all so hopeful for this trial. Maybe it was too much to ask of her little body. Maybe we will never know why it had to be this way. We need to be grateful we had what little time we did with her."

"It's just not fair. It should have been me."

"She wouldn't have survived losing you. She'd have given up."

"I don't want to live without her," I said truthfully.

"She wouldn't want you to feel that way. She would want you to live and do everything she couldn't."

He handed me her journal and smiled sadly. "Her mother read this and felt that it was meant for you. Her last words were about you and the love you shared. Keep it. Remember our November."

I held the book close to my heart and cried. I couldn't read her words now. I may never be able to but I would cherish her journal forever. They were her thoughts, her love on those pages.

The day passed slowly, every second seeming to last an eternity. Mr. and Mrs. Collins made arrangements for November's body and they promised to keep me aware of all of the arrangements for her service. I told them I wanted to speak and they simply nodded.

Night had finally fallen and I was alone in my hospital bed when the door opened and my parents walked in. I was in shock and disbelief seeing them there but the moment my mother hugged me I collapsed into the deep sadness that enveloped me.

It would be hours before I could tell them about my beautiful and loving November. I told them of her kindness on that first day and how she'd become my best friend and all of the fun things we'd spent our time doing.

"I loved her."

It was the last thing I said before I fell asleep in my mother's arms.

The day of her service dawned sunny and warm. She would have loved this weather. My father helped me tie my tie and into my sports coat. Mother handed me my knit hat, the one I'd worn the night we married.

I walked into that church, and straight to her coffin. She looked small and lifelike. I expected her to reach out for me. I reached out a shaking hand and took her hand in mine. The small diamond on her hand the only indication that she'd ever been mine. My tears fell freely as I stood with her body and spoke words of love and comfort to her. I wanted her to know that I was okay but I wasn't. I would never be okay again.

I don't know how long I'd been there when my parents and hers came and led me to our seats. The pastor spoke of a life taken too soon and how it was God's will. No loving God would have taken November from this world. She was pure and her soul was needed here.

Soon it was my turn to speak and I took a deep breath and stood up.

Behind the podium, I pulled the notes from my jacket pocket and stood staring down at her closed coffin, the red roses on it shining in the sunlight that flooded in through the windows.

"I'm Wyatt, November's husband."

I waited for the whispering to stop and people to settle down before I continued.

"The night before she left, I asked her to marry me and she said yes. We exchanged vows and were married in our eyes. And then she was gone. As quickly as she entered my life, she left it. But she left behind a man she changed with her kindness and love. Her strength gave me hope that she'd win her battle against cancer. Her laughter filled my soul with joy. She talked of wanting to ride hot air balloons and see the world from up high. She longed to swim in the ocean and see dolphins up close. She wanted to dance under the moonlight in Paris and spend nights in Italy. And I wanted to give it all to her.

She often told me she had no friends, but everyone who ever met her, fell in love with her. On the night we married I vowed to love her until my last breath and I will. I will never love anyone the way I love you November. You were the shining light that led me to find my happiness. You gave me more love in a few months than I've known in my eighteen years on this Earth.

In true November fashion, you made sure I was happy before you left. You never gave up on me and I'm so thankful that you loved me. In the words of the song you were named after…'If we could take the time to lay it on the line I could rest my head just knowin' that you were mine.'

And you were mine. You were my wife in every sense of the word. I will always reach out for you in the moonlight, always long to hold you in my arms. You were mine, body, soul and heart. And I am yours."

I looked up at the sea of faces looking at me and took another breath, then wiped my tears with the back of my hand before continuing.

"November was a pure soul, gentle and loving. She gave all of herself to make the world around her happy. She was a fighter. I had no idea how to handle being a cancer patient and she taught me with her grace and friendship. She showed me how to fight, to never give up and to always want to live.

I asked her once if she wanted to die. She said NO. She'd been crying and talking about how she didn't want to fight and I knew that she didn't mean it. So I asked her. It was then that she made the choice to fight cancer one more time. She felt everything so strongly and when she saw how hurt I was that my own parents weren't visiting, she opened her heart and sent her own father to be my stand in dad.

I think a part of me fell in love with her the moment I laid eyes on her. She was this tiny little girl with a huge personality and an attitude to match. She read voraciously, anything and everything she could get her hands on. She watched old tv shows and laughed at the silliest things. She turned me on to some of the greatest movies and music that has ever existed.

But the one thing she did the best….was love. She gave it so freely, as if she were afraid that there wouldn't be enough time for her to love enough. She spent seventeen short years on this planet and it surely wasn't enough.

I look around at all the people in this church and see your tears but I want you to know that she wouldn't want you to cry for her. She's free finally. She's free from the pain and the fear that she never gave into. She is free to run and be young. She will never grow old. She left knowing how deeply she was loved. She was happy in those last moments and that is all she ever wanted.

Every time I look up at the stars I'll know she's looking down on me and still loving me. I'll hear her whispers of love on the wind."

I stepped away from the podium and I laid my folded sheet of paper on her coffin and I kissed the beautiful pink box she laid in. My soul lay in there with her and I would forever be changed by this tiny woman I called my wife.

"I love you, November. Rest easy now my beautiful wife. We'll take it from here and continue the fight."

I felt the hands on my shoulders before I even realized that Mr. Collins had joined me. He helped me to my seat and shook my father's hand before returning to his seat.

I was numb as I listened to him and her mother speak, followed by her sister. Then one by one the nurses all spoke. Everyone talked of her gentle spirit and how they'd come to love her over the years. They spoke of how determined she was to beat this disease and how she'd changed when she'd met me.

Her mother wept quietly in the front pew, Tracy holding onto her as if her life depended on it. Mr. C, he sat stoically, his shoulders slumping from time to time as he dropped his head to wipe his tears. He couldn't keep his eyes off the photo of November that had been placed on the small stage.

In it she was laughing and running, the Autumn sunlight streaking her hair gold as leaves fell around her. She wore an old Guns N Roses tee and jeans and she looked to be about ten or so. Just before she got sick, I thought to myself.

I'd never known her without cancer and I longed to have had just one day with a healthy November. I looked around the chapel, my eyes landing on another photo of her. She was bald but that same smile lit up her face. Her love of life shone through even the hardest of times.

She hadn't wanted to fight and I knew that she'd decided to partly for her parents' sake and partly for mine. That's who she was. She wouldn't want us to worry about her as she grew weak from the cancer. So she'd chosen to fight, even if it wasn't what she'd wanted.

She'd said she didn't want to die and I had believed her. If I hadn't come into her life would she have made the same choice? I wasn't sure anymore.

Our friendship and relationship only happened because we both had cancer. Would I have even looked her way had I not gotten sick? Would she have liked the me I was before I met her?

I doubted it. I was just like my friends and they were obnoxious. I was a spoiled rich kid who didn't have any supervision and thought he was invincible.

And then.....

Cancer struck and I wound up in the same hospital and November. I remember her the day I arrived. She'd snuck out to see who was making all the noise. Of course, it was me. I'd seen the eye roll and how she'd shook her head when she laid eyes on me. She was disgusted with the way I was behaving.

I couldn't blame her. I was an ass that day. I would spend the rest of my days thanking God that she'd reached out to me when I needed her the most. I couldn't imagine going through this life without having loved November Rain Collins.

My life was better because of her. She'd taught me that you could be the sickest person in a room but you didn't have to act like it. You didn't have to let cancer bring you down. She'd taught me that it was okay to cry and be not okay but that living there wasn't an option.

Somehow, every day, she found a reason to smile and be grateful that she was alive. Even when she was facing three lonely months in isolation, she still thanked the doctors and nurses for caring for her. She still got up and got dressed every day. She never lived in sadness. Not my November.

Of course she had days where she was sad. Those days were hard for her and for all of us. You could feel the difference on the floor and with the nurses. They all worried about her. They all loved her and when she was down, the entire world went dark.

She'd grown up in a world where all she remembered was being in the hospital and being sick. She was just a little girl when she'd been diagnosed. She hadn't experienced life outside of those walls even when she was in remission. She'd been homeschooled because her immune system was so weak. She gave up everything to try to stay healthy and cancer had just come back time and time again to wipe out all of the progress that she'd made.

When she'd told me about the clinical trial, I'd believed her that it was the answer to her prayers. I'd listened to what she'd told me but I realized now that she hadn't told me the full truth.

I knew first hand that chemo was hard. I'd lived it. But what they'd done to her with chemo was beyond anything I could imagine. It had been aggressive and it had been a last resort to try to rid her body of as much of the cancer cells as possible before the trial started.

And she'd willingly done it. She had taken that poison and she'd fought the effects it had on her body valiantly. She was a warrior and she'd never let me see how hard it had been.

Looking back on that night we'd shared, I should have seen the pain she was in. I should have noticed how tired she was. I should have insisted that she stay in her room in isolation like she was instructed.

Maybe.....maybe if I had she'd still be here. Maybe I'd wake up tomorrow and be able to talk to her, to hear her laugh at my stupid jokes or to listen to her tell me about some book she was reading.

Maybe.

It was a huge word that word.

Maybe.

I wanted all of the maybes to be true. I wanted her back.

My father's hand on my arm brought me back to the reality of her funeral. I watched as members of her family lifted her coffin off the stand and carried her down the aisle. My father reached for me as I stepped out of the pew and his hand slipped away as I looked at him pleadingly.

It was the last thing I could do for her and I was going to do it if it killed me.

I stepped in beside a young man about my age and grabbed the handle of her coffin and he smiled sadly and helped me.

I carried her to that hearse and helped them slide her in. I stood there, tears falling down my face as they closed the door and in some way, they closed my heart off to anyone else.

I refused to leave the cemetery until my folks and her's forced me to. The funeral home had all but given up hope that I'd leave so they could finish their jobs. I stood there, silently staring at that pink coffin.

It held my life inside and I wasn't ready to let her go.

"Come on, Wyatt," my father urged quietly. "Her family needs to go to the reception and they won't leave until they know you're okay."

I looked back at him and I yelled.

"I. AM. NOT. OKAY."

"Damnit, son, I know that. We all know that but she's gone and you standing here like a statue is only causing more pain for her mother. Have some compassion."

"They can go. You can all go. I'm not leaving her here. She wouldn't want to be alone."

"Wyatt, I promise you we will come back after but right now, Mrs. Collins will not budge until you are in that car and on the way to their home. Please, for November, get in the car. Give her mother just a moment of peace."

I sighed heavily and looked back at November's mom. She was leaning against the black car, her face buried in her handkerchief. My heart ached for her and I knew that I had no choice but to leave November here and allow her parents to grieve for her.

I should've allowed myself the same grace but I couldn't. Not now. I blamed myself for her death. Logically I knew that it was the cancer that took her but I played a part in her death. If I had refused her request for that night. If I had insisted she stay in isolation or told the nurses what she was planning.

Maybe, just maybe, she'd still be alive and I'd get more time with her. I was torturing myself. I deserved it. Without my help, she'd still be alive.

I wanted to confess everything. I wanted to tell her parents how I was to blame but her mother was still so sad and I didn't want to add to it.

The drive to her house was long and filled with silence. My parents were trying, I had to give them that, but there wasn't anything that they could do to make this better. They couldn't throw money at this and make it go away. Though, that money had helped me get out of the hospital for the funeral. Not that anyone would have stopped me from being there. I would have walked if I had had to.

We parked in front of the house and I sat there, looking at the small house surrounded by a white picket fence. This was the house that November had grown up in. It was where she learned to walk and it was where she came when she was well. I didn't want to go in. I didn't want to see this home without her in it.

My mom opened the car door and urged me out. "Wyatt, honey, they're expecting you to make an appearance. We don't have to stay long. You have to be back at the hospital soon."

I nodded and slid out of the car. She put her arm around me and my father led the way in. I held my breath as I crossed the threshold and entered this private space that she'd lived in.

Every room had photos of November smiling in them. I studied the baby pictures in the hall, her kindergarten picture, all of the elementary ones and then there was the very first one where she had no hair.

She was still smiling and I could see that unmistakable twinkle in her eyes. I was mesmerized by that photo. I nearly jumped out of my skin when Mr. Collins put his hand on my shoulder.

"Wyatt, are you okay?"

I turned to look at him, his grief written all over his face. "No. I'm not sure I ever will be again."

"Yeah, I get that. I'm not sure any of us will ever be the same but I do believe that we will all be okay someday."

"I don't know how but I hope you're right, Mr. C."

"Wyatt, son, I don't know what to say right now. I'm still drowning in my own grief but I thought you may want something of hers other than that journal. Claire and I talked it over and she thought it would be okay for you to look around November's room and if you want to take something, you're welcome to it."

I couldn't speak so I just followed him down the hall. I don't know what I'd been expecting when he opened the door but it wasn't what I walked into.

November's room was covered in pink. There was a large queen sized bed and lots of pictures everywhere. The smiling faces of the nurses from OMHH stared back at me and my breath caught in my throat. These were her friends, the people who loved her as much as I did.

I ran my hand across the things she cherished and I felt closer to her. I sat down on her bed and I took a deep breath. I closed my eyes and I could almost feel her here with me. I could hear her voice in my head, telling me to not give up, to keep fighting. I could feel the love we'd shared.

Maybe I was losing my mind but I felt her as sure as if she were sitting here beside me. I opened my eyes and looked around the room just to make sure I wasn't dreaming. I stood up and crossed the small space over to her dresser. Hanging from the mirror was a bookmark that had a little orange kitten on it and it made me think of the time she'd told me about her cat and how much she'd missed him. I put the bookmark into my pocket and I felt as if I were going to be okay.

The rest of the day went by quickly and before long it was time for my parents to take me back to the hospital. I said my goodbyes to Mr. and Mrs. Collins and they promised to visit soon.

On the ride to the hospital my mother informed me that she planned to spend the night with me. She promised me that both her and my father were going to spend more time with me while I was in treatment. November's death had opened their eyes that they could lose me and they didn't want that to happen.

I didn't believe it fully and probably wouldn't for a very long time but if November had somehow made them open their eyes then I owed her.

The next few weeks passed agonizingly slow without November there to talk to. My mother stayed with me every single night I was in the hospital. Tomorrow I got to go home. For how long remained to be seen but my next chemo wasn't scheduled for at least a month.

My scans and MRIs were looking good. The tumor was shrinking so it looked like the treatment was working. Maybe one day soon I could say that I was cancer free or at least in remission.

Wyatt : Four years later

I stood on the front porch and knocked softly. Mr. Collins pulled me into a hug the second he opened the door.

“Wyatt, come in. Claire is going to be so thrilled to see you.”

I followed him into the house and sat down on the couch across from him. The last time I’d been here was at November's funeral. I’d stopped by and laid flowers for her before I came here. I’d needed the time to talk to her, to fill her in on all that had happened.

“Tell me how you’ve been.”

“Pretty good Mr. C. I’ve been in remission for the last two years and it looks like the tumor hasn’t grown. Of course, they can’t get it all out and I’ve had some memory loss and a little trouble with speech from time to time but I’m in therapy for that.”

“That’s wonderful to hear. We’ve kept in touch with your folks. Seems that you are all spending a lot more time together. That’s good.”

“Yes, I owe that to November.”

"She had a way of making people believe things, didn't she?"

"She sure did. I stopped by to see her earlier. She would have loved the spot you chose for her. The sunlight hits her just perfectly."

"We wanted to give her something she loved. So tell me, Wyatt, what are you up to these days?"

"School. I finally enrolled in college. I spent a year traveling with my parents and when we got back I decided I wanted to go to school. November had always talked about college and how she hated that she'd never get to go."

"What are you going to study?"

"Business. My dad wants me to intern at his corporation and learn the business. I figured it wouldn't hurt."

"That's great Wyatt. I'm so happy to hear that you're doing so well. November only ever wanted you to have a good life."

"I keep her with me all the time. I'll never forget how she changed my life. I'll always love her."

"Just don't let a memory keep you from finding love again. She would want you to be happy."

Wyatt: Ten Years later

I stopped the car and looked in the rearview mirror and smiled. She was beautiful but small, just like her namesake. I'd planned on being here sooner but life had gotten in the way but we were here now and that was all that mattered.

I got out and took her out of the car seat, setting her down and taking her small hand in mine. She wasn't the least bit concerned about where we were, she was just happy to be out and walking.

I rang the bell and waited.

Mr. and Mrs. Collins both opened the door and instantly exclaimed how beautiful my daughter was.

"November, this is Gran and Gramps C. Remember we talked about them and how we'd be coming to see them?"

She turned her little face up and looked at me then ran into Mrs. Collins' arms and hugged her close.

“She’s just precious, Wyatt,” Mr. Collins said, staring at her in disbelief. “I can’t believe how grown she is already.”

“I’m sorry we didn’t make it down sooner but work has been crazy and Macie just hasn’t been up to the trip so I had to make the time to come on my own.”

“It’s okay, son. We don’t expect you to keep coming down. Your life is different now and you need to spend time with your own family. We’re just grateful that you think of us at all.”

I watched November’s mother with my daughter and I felt a pang of sadness that she wasn’t my daughter with November. Instead, I’d named her after her because a small part of my heart just couldn’t let her go.

“She’s beautiful, Wyatt!” Mrs. Collins was all smiles and before I knew it, November and her were on the floor playing with dolls.

“I’m glad she can get to know you. Thank you. Thank you for loving me enough to let me love November.”

“Did you take her by the cemetery?””

“I did. She played with the flowers on November’s grave. She’s too little now to understand but when she’s old enough, I plan to tell her all about the woman she is named after. I’ve kept her journal and the few things I have of her’s so that my November can have them.”

“You did good, Wyatt. I know she’s looking down from Heaven and she’s happy that you’ve made a life that you can be proud of and that you found someone to love.”

“I miss her.” It was all I could say as the tears welled up in my eyes.

“Shh, don’t do that now,” Mr. Collins said. “Missing her, that’s okay but stopping your life because you miss her is silly. You gave her so much love in such a short time.”

“I still love her.”

“Just don’t let the memories interfere with the love you and Macie have. You have this beautiful little girl now, Wyatt. Don’t throw anything away on the past. Move forward and someday, you and November will be together again. She’s waiting for you to live a long and healthy life.”

My daughter and I spent the day with her honorary grandparents and she loved them and they loved her. I could feel November in their home and I was filled with love knowing that she was still around.

This should have been our happy ending but life doesn’t always work out the way you want it to. November knew that better than anyone and she’d lived her life inside a hospital but she never forgot to live every moment of it. She had brought so much love and happiness into my life. I would be forever grateful that she had taught me to love and how to be strong.

On the drive home, I told my daughter a story about a young girl who fought so bravely against a dragon named Cancer. I told her how the dragon had won the war but that the girl went out valiantly.

November cried and wanted to know why the dragon had killed the girl. I explained to her the best way that I could that sometimes the dragons win but it's how we fight that matters. She was too small to understand but someday I'd make sure that she knew. I prayed that she'd never go through anything like what November and I had when we were young but I wanted her to know that she could get through anything.

Once we were home, I laid her in her bed and kissed her sleeping face. She looked so much like her mother and it warmed my heart.

I'd met Macie five years after November died. She was small and thin, just like November had been. I'd known right away that she was the one and only person that could own a piece of my heart. As we'd become closer, I'd told her about November. She'd held me and we cried together.

One year later, we were married. She'd added a small charm with November's photo to her bouquet and I was more sure than ever that November had sent her to me. Macie healed my heart and brought me happiness.

Now here we were just a few years later with our daughter and another on the way. Life hadn't turned out quite the way I'd expected when I was just a teenager but I wouldn't change a thing. November Rain Collins had taught me so much more than I would have ever learned on my own. Every second I'd spent with her had been beautiful and I was blessed to have known her.

Someday, we will meet again and I'll be able to tell her how great my life had been. And I knew beyond a shadow of a doubt that she'd listen and be happy that I'd found love again. Until then, I'd carry on honoring the love we'd shared and keep her memory alive because she was worth everything and I loved her.

Finis.....

Made in the USA
Middletown, DE
17 August 2024

59320658R00061